Too Many Bird Books

The Story of an Intermittent Watcher

Geoffrey Dabb

Publisher: Inspiring Publishers,
P.O. Box 159, Calwell, ACT Australia 2905
Email: publishaspg@gmail.com
http://www.inspiringpublishers.com

A catalogue record for this book is available from the National Library of Australia

National Library of Australia The Prepublication Data Service

Author: Geoffrey Dabb
Title: Too Many Bird Books
Genre: Non-fiction

Paperback ISBN: 978-1-922920-61-4
eBook ISBN: 978-1-922920-63-8

The Northern Shoveler, an occasional celebrated rarity in Australia, at Kelly Swamp, Canberra, in 2019, and as presented for book-reading duck-watchers of the northern hemisphere by Audubon (1830), Gould (1871), Stewart (1853), Frank Chapman & Chester Reed (1903), and Robin Hill (1987).

About the covers

Front cover: This does not need much explanation. The bird shown is clearly grappling with too many bird books, despite this species of pelican being a world record-holder as regards bill length. The authority on this point is *The Bird Almanac* (David Bird, 2004 - see his photo, by Barbara Allan, at p.139). The *Almanac* awards the title thus: 'absolute longest bill: Australian Pelican at 47 cm'.

Back cover: The base photo is of an Indian Peacock in flight. A certain amount of symbolism has crept into this composition. The book connection is provided by the images of Australian Magpie and Bennett's Cassowary, both from John Gould's famous volumes on Australian birds (although his cassowary lives in New Guinea). The human/bird figure, also from New Guinea, has exercised his or her right, in this age of self-identification, to be a bird. The book-carrying Watcher is from an evocative metal figure, not able to be attributed to the sculptor by name, unfortunately. Restraint has been exercised to avoid the adding of too many other birds, but a few have got in. You might see a Dollarbird and a 'Pied Coot', the latter coming to mind at any mention of black-and-white birds. You might also notice Australia's currently most mysterious species, the erratically-wandering painted-snipe. The answer to the riddle has not yet been disclosed, but there is speculation among experts that it might be 'the Australian Constitution', the part about swooping cyclists being an exaggeration.

Preface to the First Edition

Actually, this is, and quite possibly will remain, the only edition. I do not anticipate a long book-generating career. When I told Andrew Isles, the seductive bird-book vendor, that I intended to write a book, his comment was, 'Ah, yes—that's what we call vanity publishing'. If you bought this book, you would not have paid what it cost to produce. It has probably also entailed a disproportionate amount of time and effort. But then, in retrospect, in the lives of few people are time and effort applied to things in the correct proportions.

It is difficult to make a well-proportioned list of all the people who should be acknowledged. Neil Murray allowed me to use photos from the wonderful collection in his self-published *Education Officer T.P.N.G.* (2010). Robin Hill, Hugh Beggs, and Andrew Black helped with other images. Encouragers include Russell McGregor, who is going to write a cultural history of birdwatching in Australia. The fact is, several hundred people have each told me something interesting about birds. To mention just friends in Canberra, there is Robin Hide, Richard Allen, Jack Holland, Jenny Bounds, Michael Lenz, Penny Olsen, Leo Joseph, Joe Forshaw… There is little point in going on. Each further name mentioned extends the circle of names that should not be left out. Several people are mentioned in the following pages. I should also thank my family for being there in the background, generally supportive, sometimes baffled, but supportive.

What this book is about

It is about birds, but particularly about bird books. You might have noticed there are a lot of them out there, with more arriving on the bookshelves all the time. Perhaps at some future point the flow will slacken, as people make more use of digital offerings. I might be wrong. There might be thousands more books still to come. However, I think it's quite possible that the main period covered by this book, roughly my own lifetime, say from the Second World War to the 2020s, will come to be seen as the great age of popular printed bird literature. During that time, books were generally inexpensive, and many, certainly not all, were aimed at the general public. This particular book, then, is in part the story of recent bird literature from the viewpoint of a bird-book addict. That might seem to be a slightly disparaging self-description, but, to borrow the memorable phrase of John Lennon, a well-known musical performer from the same period, I'm not the only one.

Contents

TOO MANY BIRD BOOKS: the story of an intermittent Watcher

Buffy: I've got a better idea. *You* slay them.

Rupert: No! A Slayer slays, A Watcher…

Buffy: Watches?

Rupert: Yes … er, no…

- *Buffy the Vampire Slayer,* Season One

Prologue

A recent illustrative experience of looking up things about birds, in books, and digitally.

After I had finished writing what I intended to say in this book, I thought of including a picture of a carving I'd acquired in New Guinea more than 50 years ago. The subject was a bird standing on a pig. For the first time I gave serious consideration to which species it was (the bird, not the pig). From the crest and head, the bird must be one of the Goura pigeons, large, crowned pigeons that feed on the ground. They are New Guinea's most spectacular contribution to the world's pigeon fauna, being 'almost the size of a turkey'. (That is according to Tom Iredale, for one, in his *Birds of New Guinea*.) William Dampier was the first European to record a specimen in 1700, 'a stately Land-Fowl', he said.

My carved bird has a longish bill with a hooked end. To see if this is accurately represented, I check the online photos in the vast Cornell Lab photo library and other available pictures, no doubt some from zoos. There's quite a bit of variation, but a few individuals have a bill shape like my carved bird. The associated eBird website also shows that you'd need to do quite a bit of work to tick all four Goura species in one day. The popular ticking locations are, for the Western species, on Waigeo Island (Indonesia) and, for Sclater's, the relatively recent accommodations around once-remote Kiunga on the upper Fly River.

I also wanted an interesting bird image to show alongside the carving, preferably something early with no copyright issue. (Speaking of early, William Dampier had managed a drawing with his report from 1700, but I can't find a useable version of that.) I have a small hand-colored picture by Edward Lear, which I thought I would use, after I'd put a source to it. This brings me to what I want to draw attention to here, the great trove of historic published material you can find now in digitised holdings, for example those of the Biodiversity Heritage Library (BHL).

The Scottish naturalist William Jardine (1800–1874) performed a remarkable publishing feat by producing something called *The Naturalist's Library*, 40 volumes with hand-colored plates. Fourteen volumes, issued 1853–1855, deal with birds. For a collector of old books the complete set is currently for sale in Sydney for about AUD10,000. However, the complete set might also be viewed digitally through BHL. Through this, I find my little Edward Lear drawing of the stately Goura pigeon. There it is at the end of the pigeon volume. The page size is much smaller than the bird, 103mm x 130mm.

Carved wooden figure of Goura pigeon standing on a pig. Acquired in New Guinea in 1960s. At right is the Edward Lear drawing of a Goura pigeon for the *Naturalist's Library* (not a native of Java, as stated in the text by P. J. Selby).

The work of the flower painter Ellis Rowan is mentioned in a later chapter. There is something of a mystery about when and where she painted her bird subjects. Among Ellis's watercolours in the National Library of Australia (NLA) are two of Goura pigeons. Curiously, they are two different species. In each, Ellis gave as much attention to the lacy crest as she gave to the detail of her floral subjects.

The spectacular heads of Ellis Rowan's Goura pigeons photographed from the originals in the NLA. The one on the left is the north coast species, Victoria Crowned Pigeon *Goura victoria*. It is not known where these were painted. If painted from life they should have shown a large pigeon iris, conspicuously bright red in each case.

The scanning of books by BHL, or its agents, sometimes made use of different sets of volumes held in different places, sometimes of multiple series for the same work. One scanned set of *The Naturalist's Library* bears the bookseller's sticker 'S. Sissons' of Worksop, a village near Sheffield, UK. That set was evidently bought for a school, because each volume has the inscription 'Bought out of disorder fines', with a date from '25. 11. 54' to '25. 1. 58'. This, it seems to me, is an indication that the *Naturalist*'s series was relatively inexpensive – or that the fines were unusually punitive, or that the disorder was at a St Trinian's level. So I infer that the *Naturalist's Library* was at the opposite end of the price scale from John Gould's lavish productions of about the same time.

I

Beginnings. I go to New Guinea.

I begin with a moment in a childhood in Geelong, Victoria, Australia, not long after 'the war'. The precautionary air-raid trenches had been filled in on the grounds of North Geelong primary school. I was particularly excited, more than the other screaming children, when they flushed the Barn Owl[1] from its roost in the corner of the shelter-shed. This makes me think of that question you sometimes hear, in one form or other: what kind of disorder of the personality separates a child from the mainstream by turning them so early towards an interest in birds?

Most schoolchildren in those days were likely to be taught something about birds, more than today's children. As required by the curriculum of the day, there were 'nature study' classes where the subject might be the difference between a Scarlet Robin and a Flame Robin. For a still earlier generation, Frank Tate, Director of Education, had written in a flowery introduction to Leach's *Australian Bird Book* (1911) 'nature-study is bringing our boys and girls into kindlier relationships with our birds'.

Many State-school teachers had done their early teaching in rural Victoria, perhaps at a school in the Mallee or in Gippsland. They'd been able to pick up a few points about rural birds. However, I remember one piece of unsound teacherly advice. A flock of small bright green parrots was twittering and feeding in the blossom at the top of the schoolyard gum trees. I think now they were one of the smaller lorikeets – or perhaps Swift Parrots. I was told they were 'budgerigars'. For years I had the wrong idea about where you were likely to find real Budgerigars.

---

[1] I have now mentioned a bird. It is 'Barn Owl' and not 'barn owl' because it is used as the name of a recognized species. On the other hand, I would write 'parrot' and not 'Parrot', because that is an ordinary word and not the name of a species. However, it is difficult to be consistent about this. For example, in a paragraph just ahead, I believe the schoolteacher said 'budgerigars' and not 'Budgerigars', because he did not know, and probably did not care, that a Budgerigar was a species. It depends on the context. I hope the apparent inconsistencies that follow will not be irritating to the reader.

Near the end of our street, projecting a modest distance into Corio Bay, was a wooden structure known as 'Wood's Jetty'. Many days were spent trying to catch small fish from the end of it. The jetty was named for Percy Wood, a butcher who had owned a launch used in connection with his ship provisioning business. In his retirement, Mr Wood wrote a bird column in the *Geelong Advertiser*, identifying himself as 'PJW'. He lived around the corner from our street, at his house on The Esplanade, with a view over the bay.

My mother arranged for me to visit Mr Wood on two or three occasions. He had promised, according to my mother, that if I took an interest in nature I would never be lonely. He was certainly a good source of information. In response to my questions, he explained that those green rosellas were the young of the red ones, and those large brown gulls, called 'mollymawks' by some people, were the young of the large black and white gulls. Also, that the 'blue crane' was not really a crane.

Books, sometimes more interesting than birds even, are going to be a large part of this story. If I am going to talk about books, I should give some idea of my perspective, by telling you how I came to experience them. Here is an early book moment. Mr Wood was explaining the difference between the spoonbill with the yellow legs and bill and the one with the black legs and bill. He reached into a bookcase to take down one of a set of large books to show me a picture. I realised years later that I was looking at a set of Gregory Mathews's *Birds of Australia*, with its hand-coloured lithographs. In 1996, Trevor Pescott published a different kind of book, *Geelong's Birdlife in Retrospect*, with selections of articles by PJW, from 1945 to 1958, and some information about the life of Mr Wood himself.

My father was overseas during much of the 1940s. My mother sometimes took the family to visit my father's parents at Upwey, in the Dandenongs on the other side of Melbourne. That was a good place for birds. The trip took most of a day and entailed travel by various public conveyances, including a then fully operational Puffing Billy on its narrow-gauge rail track. I remember looking out at the small orchard from my grandparents' deck with a little pair of brass-encased binoculars, at one of those bird sights that stays with you, and by itself could set you off on a watching career. It was a male Golden Whistler.

I used to go to school on a tram. The distance was less than a mile, and occasionally I would walk one way. This took me past a suburban park with a stand of pines. At that spot, I was introduced to the terror of attack by (Australian) magpie, with that alarming bill-crack. In the nesting season I would take a longer route to avoid that park.

My parents gave me a copy of *What Bird Is That?* with Neville Cayley's illustrations of, it was said, all Australian bird species. A book to be treasured, but most of the birds I saw were introduced ones, and not in the early Cayley editions. No sparrows, no blackbirds, no starlings, not even the goldfinches that built their little nests in our apricot trees. Three other common birds were missing. No Song Thrush, an active bird in our garden, usually seen scratching away in the leaf litter under the shrubs. And no 'dove'. A neighbour had a massive, towering dark cypress, the home of several members of this species (now 'Spotted Dove'). In their display flights they would racket up noisily, before making that steep downward glide. And no 'pigeon', the familiar *Columbia livia*, a seriously neglected species, in my view. I once kept some pigeons. I have recently looked into the story behind its abundance in Australian towns.[2]

There was a small amount of egg-collecting. Apart from its bay, Geelong is surrounded by treeless plains and hills, with some exotic plantings in the town and on the suburban fringe, but little real bushland. I used to ride around a lot on my bicycle, although it was a long ride to get anywhere of much interest from a bird viewpoint. I sometimes pedaled along the Ballarat Road, up the hill past 'Morongo', the school attended by my sisters. A bit further on through a gate into a paddock was a single, large, bird-planted African Boxthorn standing on the fence-line between bare paddocks. In this were a half-dozen bulky nests of House Sparrows. I extracted the contents of these with difficulty. An exotic bird species in an exotic plant in a man-made landscape. Speaking of Ballarat, I was sent there to stay with friends for a week. In those days it had a picturesque lake, with paddle steamers, and white swans you could feed.

My parents built a beach house at Torquay. This was not on the interesting surf beach side from where the coastal scrub ran down past Bell's Beach to Anglesea. It was almost the last house, then, certainly not now, on the Geelong side. To the east, sheep paddocks, marshy grassland, and sand dunes extended across to Breamlea and on to Barwon Heads. I spent a lot of time walking over that area looking for anything of interest. I would occasionally

---

[2] My conclusions may be found in *Canberra Bird Notes* 44:3 Dec 2019 http://canberrabirds.org.au/wp-content/uploads/2020/01/CBN-44-3-final.pdf

flush pipits and quail and small groups of bright green ground-feeding parrots. With my Cayley, I worked out that these were Orange-bellied Parrots that bred in Tasmania, long gone now, I would think, from that particular refuge.

Then came the years as a day-student at Geelong Grammar. This is situated on an arm of Corio Bay. In the early 1900s, boys would be taken to the school by boat from Geelong. Two ancient buses operated by the school were used in my time. The small bay was known as 'the Grammar School Lagoon', but is now 'Limeburner's Lagoon State Nature Reserve', part of the Werribee-Avalon Ramsar site and therefore A WETLAND OF INTERNATIONAL IMPORTANCE. ('Ramsar' is the name of the place in Iran where an international treaty was signed relating to wetlands conservation.)

There were some noteworthy birds on and around the lagoon: pelicans, spoonbills, oystercatchers, terns, but not the great flocks of migratory shorebirds you find some kilometres away at the Werribee sewage treatment complex. White-fronted Chats were common in the saltmarsh vegetation. The wide flat paddocks around the school were only occasionally productive. Seasonally, the fences beside the great lines of cypress plantings might provide perches for families of those Scarlet or Flame Robins, or occasional Horsfield's Bronze-Cuckoos. Sometimes you would see a Swamp Harrier or Brown Falcon. The common 'crow' was the Little Raven.

Occasionally, a flock of Banded Lapwings could be seen. Another book needs to be mentioned here. Horatio Wheelwright (1815–1865) had come to Australia with the gold-rushes. He became a commercial shooter of game for the markets, living a roving, camping existence within 40 miles of Melbourne. He has left us *Bush Wanderings of a Naturalist* (1861), an account of the wildlife of the area that was worth shooting, and of some that was not. In its pages we can recognize the following species: 'The *Plover of the Plains* is about one-third less than the spur-wing, congregates in large flocks, and is, I think, altogether a commoner bird in its peculiar localities.' He adds: 'Neither of these birds are strictly game, but we could often sell them at 1*s.* and 1*s.* 6.*d* per couple.'

A quickening of interest came with the few months spent at the Geelong Grammar outpost known as 'Timbertop', near Mansfield and not far from Mount Buller. This was the first year this bush campus was in operation. It was in high-country forest, with a different set of birds. Boys were encouraged to take hikes, including overnight camping at the weekends.

I was one of a small gang of boys that devoted much free time to looking for interesting birds, particularly nesting ones. One quarry was the Satin Flycatcher, another the Rufous Fantail. In retrospect, a large part of the motivation was the interest of one of us, Hugh Beggs, in bird photography.

Another of our group was a good climber. He had the job of tying Hugh's bellows camera to a branch near a nest. It would be activated from several metres' distance, for just one shot, by a length of fishing line attached to the trigger. The results, as I recall, were surprisingly good, in the form of large black-and-white prints. Hugh was of a family in rural western Victoria. One of his sisters married Malcolm Fraser. He knew more about birds than I did. Highlights of the career of a watcher include not only encounters with notable birds but talking to people who know more about them than you do. Unfortunately, at Timbertop I broke a leg tobogganing down a steep muddy slope and spent months on crutches with a leg-length plaster cast.

Then, after school, four years at Melbourne University. This can be labelled as one of my no-time-for-birds periods. There were too many other things going on. I do, however, have two bird memories. One is walking on a brilliant sunny morning from Queen's College to a lecture, and seeing three Galahs feeding on the university oval. These days, such a sight might seem commonplace, when Galahs can be found with terns and gulls on Australia's southern beaches. However, in the 1950s they were unusual in the centre of Melbourne. We now know that that was a period of range expansion of this species, when it advanced out of its home in the semi-arid zone. Another bird experience was putting up with the Common Mynas noisily copulating on the college lawns just before and during the exam season. That species was one of the most common in suburban Melbourne.

In 1962, having qualified as a lawyer, I was working in Melbourne in a small practice conducted by a well-known criminal courts advocate, Ray Dunn, and uncertain where life would take me. I saw an advertisement for a government legal position in the Territory of Papua and New Guinea. I thought that two years there would offer me some adventure before resuming my career as a lawyer in Melbourne. The pay and conditions seemed quite generous.

There was a little more to it than that. I was of an age when people were around who had 'been in New Guinea during the war'. Geelong Grammar had a connection with the

Martyrs School at Popondetta. We knew a family whose son had been a patrol officer. I knew a law student who had done some vacation work in Port Moresby. One of my law lecturers, Professor David Derham, had recently made a visit there to recommend changes to the legal system, and had spoken about what an interesting place it was. Over the years, I had read articles in the (American) *National Geographic Magazine* that made New Guinea a place for which 'interesting' was too weak an adjective. An article in an old issue (April 1953) was 'New Guinea's Rare Birds and Stone Age Men' by an American ornithologist, E. Thomas Gilliard.

Given how close Papua New Guinea is, and its past close association with Australia, it is surprising that Australians today know so little about that country. Confusingly, 'New Guinea' has different meanings. It is a name of (a) the single large island now divided between Indonesia and PNG, and (b) the former Australian Trust Territory, taking in part of the main island and a few other islands, e.g. New Britain, Manus and Bougainville, and (c) a common way of referring, as herein, non-specifically, to New Guinea *and* the former Papua (e.g. 'I've been up in New Guinea'). 'Papua' is (a) the former 'British New Guinea', later an Australian territory of that name (administered after World War 2 with adjoining 'New Guinea') and (b) because it is the Malay/Indonesian name for the large island, also used in the names of Indonesian provinces on and near that island. The present name of the country formerly administered by Australia is 'Papua New Guinea'.

Myself when younger, at my grand-parents' garden, in bushland at the outskirts of the village of Upwey in the Dandenongs. My grandfather had comic sculptures and other whimsical creations around the garden. The impressions of my hands and feet, when even younger, are preserved in the concrete at the top of the arch.

Right. On a week-end hike at Timbertop. From left, Roger the Climber, Hugh Beggs, and myself. The photographer is a fourth boy who has just demonstrated his axe skills on the severed tree.

Photo of a Yellow Robin at the nest. The photo was taken by a camera placed near the nest, and triggered with a length of fishing line. This snap from Hugh's album was rephotographed and sent to me by phone.

Above - Port Moresby in 1959, from a photo by Neil Murray from Paga Hill. The Top and Bottom Pubs are on the main street. Hanuabada village and the government headquarters at Konedobu are in the distance, along or near the harbour edge .
Below - A military map of Port Moresby hinterland from the end of World War 2, still useful in 1960s: 1. Town area; 2. Jackson Drome (present airport); 3. Ward's Drome (present government centre); 4. Bomana area; 5. Waigani Swamp.

II

To Port Moresby, and beyond

The flight to Port Moresby in 1962 was an overnight run in a lumbering DC6, operated on alternate days by Ansett's 'Golden Orchid Service' and TAA's 'Sunbird Service'. You left Brisbane at midnight, and landed at Jackson airfield as the rising sun gave a view of the looming Owen Stanley range.

Basic facts about the Territory of Papua and New Guinea at that time: total population about two million, expatriates (mainly Australians) employed in the government about 5,000, population of Port Moresby about 20,000. PNG now has a population approaching 10 million, Port Moresby about 400,000.

Port Moresby in 1962, before air-conditioned buildings, had, in some of its corners, a decadent, rum-drinking atmosphere, a kind of Lord Jim, dregs-of-the-South-Seas feel. This was evident in the old town area rather than in the newer residential suburbs. An example was the Hotel Moresby, the 'bottom pub', by contrast with the 'top pub' (cleaner, more comfortable, more fashionable). The 'Snakepit Bar' in the bottom pub had rattan chairs and bar-stools and tired ceiling fans and a concrete floor, periodically mopped over or hosed out. 'Locals' were not allowed to consume alcohol until November 1962. The manager wore slightly dirty whites and ran side-businesses as off-course bookie (for Australian race meetings) and croc-skin dealer. Being a Queenslander, he liked eating mud-crab. The best way to get this, he said, was to walk around Koki market in the early morning, shouting 'bava? bava?'. The sleeping quarters upstairs, my home for two weeks, opened onto a wide, open verandah and had musty mosquito-nets.

Port Moresby has a dry-tropics climate rather like Townsville in north Queensland. Its surrounding hills and valleys are clothed with vegetation of the savannah type, until you travel beyond the rain shadow zone, and enter some real rain forest. A good description of the setting, and of the bird life as it was in the 1960s, may be found in Roy Mackay's useful little volume *The Birds of Port Moresby and District* (1970). According to this, 364 species had been recorded in the area up to November 1968.

The birds that soon came to attention when I lived in the comfortable single quarters on the slopes behind Ela Beach were the following, names as given in the Mackay book (and in the current Australian list): Rainbow Lorikeet, Papuan Greybird (White-bellied Cuckoo-shrike), Papuan Friar Bird (Silver-crowned Friarbird?), Yellow-tinted Honeyeater, Green Figbird (Australasian Figbird), Fawn-breasted Bowerbird, and Little Starling (Singing Starling).

You could drive safely along unsealed, former military roads in the savannah hinterland. These might take you past the site of the future University of Papua New Guinea – and of the future centre of national administration. You would come across old wartime airfields. Recalling one of them, the postal address of future government offices became 'Ward's Strip'. Common bird species were mainly what you could find in north Queensland: Black-backed Butcherbird, White-breasted Woodswallow, Lemon-bellied Flycatcher, Blue-winged Kookaburra, Forest Kingfisher and Pheasant Coucal (a kind of ground-dwelling cuckoo: 'What's that pheasant-type bird that runs along the side of the road?' people would ask). A conspicuous small bird in the kunai (tall reed-like grass) was the 'Pied Chat' (*Saxicola caprata* – not a close relative of the chat of Limeburner's Lagoon).

There were no birds of paradise in Port Moresby suburbs. I occasionally saw a Magnificent Riflebird when exploring margins of lowland wet forest. The place to see a Raggiana Bird of Paradise was the Sogeri plateau about 35 km by road from the Port Moresby town area. A schoolteacher at Sogeri high school 1958–1962 was Neil Murray who has produced a valuable photographic record of that area at that time, *Education Officer T.P.N.G* (self-published, 2010). Neil told me recently: 'There were lots of birds of paradise around Sogeri in those days. They were very noisy and easily seen every day. One even made a nest in the small mango tree in front of my house.' I became friends of a family on a rubber plantation, who regularly had the birds there.

A problem was that, before Mackay's book, there were *no helpful books* to tell you what birds were out there. The Cayley only covered Australian birds with little information about occurrence in New Guinea. I had a copy of a 1941 list by the famous American ornithologist Ernst Mayr, and a bare list it was, not even English names. The biggest tease was a two-volume *Birds of New Guinea* (1956) by Tom Iredale, former assistant to Gregory Mathews. His wife, Lilian Medland, had provided illustrations of 347 birds. Unfortunately, both text and illustrations seemed designed for the museum worker rather than an observer in the field. Some of the illustrations were poor representations of a bird in real life. Moreover, details of distribution were lacking.

Another book was Ernst Mayr's *Birds of the South-west Pacific*, said to be Mayr's 'popular contribution to ornithology'. I now have two copies of this, my old one published in 1945 and the reissued paperback from 1978, printed in Japan, ironically given that the first edition was prompted by US engagement in the Pacific war. In this 'popular contribution', Mayr, despite vast New Guinea experience (as shown by the 1941 taxonomic list), did not attempt to cover New Guinea birds. The birds covered were those in a south-west Pacific 'rough triangle'. '[M]any of the more common species of these islands are widespread and are also found in the Solomon Islands or Melanesia *(sic)*. It is therefore believed that this handbook will also be useful to visitors to New Guinea.' The fact was that the Cayley was more useful in New Guinea. My consequent frustration probably aggravated a serious disease, an insatiable appetite for illustrated bird books.

In the 1950s, those large, popular 'birds of the world' books had begun to appear. In the hope they would help with New Guinea birds, I had bought two in Melbourne to take with me. One was *Birds of the World* (1961) by Oliver Austin, illustrations by Arthur Singer. Not a lot of help in New Guinea, but the quality of those bold paintings (see the Golden Whistler, for example) was enough by itself to create enthusiasm for birds. The other was *Living Birds of the World* (1958) by E. Thomas Gilliard. Later, I found that Fisher and Peterson in their own *World of Birds* (1964) described those two earlier books as the outstanding examples of that kind of thing. Both those books gave some understanding of how all those new birds in New Guinea fitted in to a world-wide scheme of classification, without helping with identification. At the end of 1963, I visited Sydney in connection with two appeals to the High Court, and made another search of the bookshops, but with little success.

My work in New Guinea for the first four years entailed regular circuit travel as the prosecutor with a Supreme Court party that included judge, associate, and defending barrister. The inclusion of the last-named was a result of Professor Derham's recommendations. The court party would visit provincial centres, often by DC3 aircraft, and, using smaller, weather-dependent aircraft, some quite remote outstations. There was a lot of work in the highlands as a result of axe violence and payback killings. I had one case at Kainantu where the principal defendant was killed just outside the court with axes that two witnesses had brought along for the purpose.

Regrettably, there was little court work in the islands of Milne Bay District, in the east of 'Papua'. I enjoyed two circuits there where the court travelled in leisurely fashion on a government boat. There are no gulls in PNG waters, but you would occasionally see terns bobbing along on coconuts or other floating debris. We anchored overnight by a small island (Goodenough), whose peak out-topped the highest point in mainland Australia.

Typical birds at an outstation included birds you might see in Australia: Rainbow Bee-eater, Sacred and Forest Kingfishers, Willie Wagtail. Schach's (now Long-tailed) Shrike (a true shrike, not something you find in Australia) was quite common in the highlands. The officer in charge at Wabag had a tame Kokomo (hornbill) and near his garden I saw a Belford's Melidectes, a large honeyeater identified from the Iredale. While talking to the mining warden at Wau, I saw a Hooded Pitohui through the open window. From a small aircraft you could sometimes see large birds flying low over the rain-forest canopy, such as Kokomos and white cockatoos and pigeons.

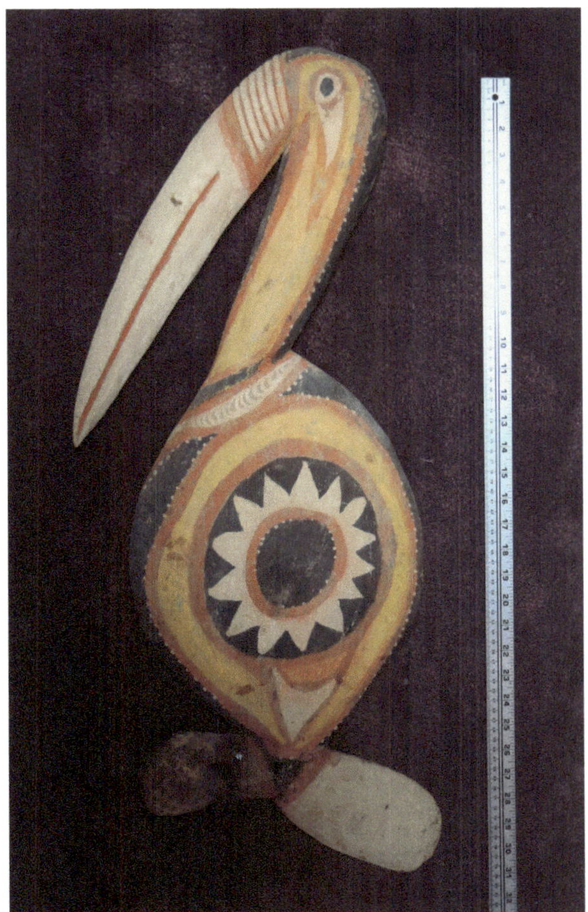

The Kokomo, being the one species of hornbill in New Guinea, is a familiar motif. I still have this carving, acquired at Maprik in about 1966. Displayed as a wall hanging, it has had falls from various heights, occasionally losing its feet.

Other sightings remembered from those circuit days: shorebirds feeding across the glutinous black mudflats at Daru, near the Fly River estuary; a boldly marked Long-tailed Buzzard circling over one of the wartime airfields near Popondetta; Oriental Pratincoles and Blue-tailed Bee-eaters hawking for insects over the old Rabaul airfield, near a smouldering Matupit volcano; the striking Pied Harriers hunting over the kunai, that you would see on the drive from Goroka to Lae down the Markham valley; captive New Guinea Harpy-Eagles in the aviary at the District Commissioner's house at Mount Hagen.

Madang was a favourite port of call: lush and scenic, with a lazy tropical tempo, and opportunities for short picturesque strolls or coastal drives. The court-house, by a tidal lagoon, was built from bush materials. On one occasion the court party took a leisurely boat trip across Astrolabe Bay to view a crime scene at a coconut plantation. On a visit in 1963, in the bar of the Madang Hotel, I came across Neptune Beresford Newcombe Blood. It would be easy here to be diverted into giving undue space to a notable part of the history of Australians in New Guinea, their activities in the highlands, particularly the Wahgi Valley. That story is recounted in *Adam in Plumes* (1954) by Colin Simpson.

In short, for present purposes, Nep, or Ned Blood as sometimes known, had been an army officer serving in the wartime administration. After the war, he was based in the Mount Hagen area. He had an interest in natural history, and collected a number of bird of paradise skins, expecting these to be of scientific interest. He also collected live birds. As he described his live-bird collecting to me, the birds were generally found in island clumps of trees. He would deploy a number of villagers up into the trees with sticks. The bird would be denied a perch in any tree, and would eventually flutter to the ground where it could be captured. Blood said he had sent 'baskets of skins' down to the Australian Museum in Sydney. It was these that had excited Iredale's interest in New Guinea birds, and led to his *Birds of Paradise and Bower Birds* (1950).

In that book, Iredale warmly acknowledges Blood's contribution. He names a species for Blood, *Paradisea bloodi*, now regarded as a hybrid. 'One of the most beautiful of all the problematic forms that have been found in New Guinea is the present species dedicated to the finder Captain N. B. Blood, whose enthusiasm has opened a new page in the story of Paradise Birds and Bower Birds. Single-handed he has secured more kinds of these birds than most of the huge expensive expeditions have brought back.'

A further part of the story is told in *Adam in Plumes*. Through his work with birds of paradise, Nep Blood met E. J. L. (later Sir Edward) Hallstrom and suggested what became the 'Hallstrom Trust Livestock Station and Zoological Gardens' in the Wahgi Valley. Blood was the first manager of the station. The live bird of paradise collection came under the management of Fred Shaw Mayer, a long-time collector of wild life in New Guinea, known as 'Masta Pijin'. He was still at Nondugl when I visited there. For visitors, he would waggle a finger and make clucking noises to cause a bird to display. Many photos of displaying birds were obtained by that method, with captive birds. Later the collection at Nondugl was moved to Baiyer River, where Roy Mackay became manager.

There was another development on that same Madang visit. Made aware of my interest in birds, Nep Blood said 'and there's the bird man over there', indicating a middle-aged person who looked like an accountant. This was E. Thomas Gilliard who was putting the final touches to a book on New Guinea birds. I came across him later, sitting at an outside table and shuffling some black and white prints for the new book. I joined him at dinner that night. This was intensely interesting for me. Here was the author not only of my *Living Birds of the World* but also of 'Rare Birds and Stone Age Men' (the *National Geographic* article).

Rand and Gilliard's *Handbook of New Guinea Birds* was published in 1967. In the introduction, one could read: 'This volume makes no pretence to being a "field guide" in the modern sense. There are no experts in field identification in this area and resident naturalists are few and scattered.' I was interested in the treatment of English names: 'A vernacular (English) name is provided for each species. These are almost all "manufactured" for most of these birds have no current English name.' There was a tendency to use the genus name as the noun in the English name, e.g. 'Slender-billed Meliphaga' for what is (or was) called in Australia 'Graceful Honeyeater'.

Sadly, Gilliard himself had died before publication, at the age of 53. A couple of years later, I came across a journal extract in which Gilliard described his bird-collecting activities in 1948 in the Port Moresby hinterland. He had been making field studies 'for a Rouna Falls habitat group for Whitney Memorial Hall in the American Museum'. Years later, on visits to New York, I would make a point of visiting the AMNH to gaze at that evocative diorama. It was adorned with an interesting but unlikely assembly of birds. There was a great background painting of the view down the Laloki Gorge, with Hombron Bluff to one side and, with a little artistic licence, Port Moresby nestling under Paga Hill in the distance.

III

To Europe, and back to New Guinea

Contrary to my initial plan for a two-year stay, I was enjoying life in New Guinea and had decided to stay there for a while. In 1965, I went on leave for six months. The *Ellinis* was a Greek-flag ex-Matson-Liner that plied between Australia and Europe. In January that year, it made a call at Port Moresby when several expatriate residents took advantage of the opportunity to get on board and take a direct route to the northern hemisphere. I was booked to the end-point of the voyage at Naples, with no firm onward plans, but a general intention of going on to London. A London-based girlfriend from Melbourne days cabled that she would meet the ship in Naples, which happened. I remember that she liked the Beatles. (I preferred Dylan, myself.) At a pensione on Capri, the proprietario made a point of putting on the television to show us Winston Churchill's funeral in progress. Naturally, he expected us to be interested.

I planned to travel by road as destinations came to mind, so I went into the Fiat outlet in Naples and bought a small Fiat 850 off the showroom floor. I had to stay in Italy to wait for tourist plates, so the girlfriend got on the train at Milan, back to London and the Beatles. This was the beginning of a long drive, usually alone, around the rural areas of Europe.

I had a large pair of binoculars and a small book, *A Field Guide to the Birds of Britain and Europe*, by Peterson, Mountfort and Hollom, still in the original edition from 1954. I still have the book. This was indeed 'a field guide in the modern sense'. There was nothing like it then for Australian birds. Its stated purpose was 'to show … how to distinguish, at reasonable distance, all the species of birds inhabiting or visiting Great Britain and the European continent'. A great advantage was that it had small maps indicating the range for each species.

I must say immediately that my total of ticks, accumulated over some 10,000 km, is quite paltry. I have no doubt I saw many more species than I recorded. I was very cautious with the warblers and pipits. A competent watcher would have improved on my tally at almost any spot where I unsheathed my binoculars. However, my main aim was not a long list but to see new birds.

Some highlights: the fulmars and puffins on the cliffs at Dunnet Head; the Kittiwakes with regulation 'dipped in ink' wingtips behind the cork-screwing fishing trawler in The Minch; a Red Kite over fields in the Welsh hills; the Red Grouse in the heather near Balmoral Castle; the Bullfinch in a bare tree in my uncle's garden at The Hague (he was an Australian posted there); the predictable birds in the olive groves of Andalusia (Great-spotted Cuckoo, Bee-eater, Roller, Little Owl, Woodchat Shrike); the flocks of Pallid Swifts making screaming circuits around the old buildings of Seville.

Naturally, there were vivid moments unrelated to birds: being locked in an old fort in Pamplona after closing time; being locked *out* of my fort-like small hotel in Sheffield and spending a freezing night in the car; taking part in the catch of a huge haul of Lythe ('Pollock' in English) and trying to sell it house-to-house in Portree (not a popular fish there, I found); a currency misunderstanding in Berlin at Checkpoint Charlie; an undistinguished round of golf at St Andrews. At that time, this was a public course where you could roll up, hire clubs, and play a round for green fees, on one of the four links courses.

On one leg of the flight back from Europe, I called again at Cairo, having already done the 'quick trip' there, while the *Ellinis* passed through the Suez Canal. Under the influence of *The Alexandria Quartet* (1957–1960), a literary feat only slightly concerned with birds, I spent a couple of days in Alexandria. I went there by train, and back to Cairo by the desert bus. I don't remember many birds, except the kites. I do remember seeing Lake Mariut (Mareotis), scene of the duck-shooting episode in *Justine*. I later acquired a book, *Sport in Egypt* (1938) by J. Wentworth Day, foreword by H.M. King Farouk. (This gave helpful phrases rendered in Arabic: 'Wrap yourself up in something black'; 'Did the pellets get you in the leg?'; 'You can keep the coot. I do not want them.') The chapter on Lake Mariut ('A Wonder Lake of Sport') recites the duck species making up one bag, amounting to '58 head, rather above average which is 40 to 50 on a good day'. At about the same period, the bag of Darley, Lawrence Durrell's central character, was disappointing. 'Eight brace no good', said his gun-bearer.

By late July, I was back in Port Moresby, with the Fiat arriving a little later containing my consignment of bird books. I had spent too much time at Foyles bookstore, Charing Cross

Road, acquiring, for example, showing here my desperation to have something relevant to New Guinea: a) the 1899 'Birds' volume (1959 reprint) of the *Cambridge Natural History* (price, an excessive £5/10/-), b) *The Birds of Borneo* (1960) by Bertram Smythies, and c) a book by someone called Meinertzhagen (more on this below). These still sit, rarely consulted, on my bookshelf.

The Chief Justice, Sir Allan Mann, had a keen interest in orchids, anthropology, birds, and in fact just about everything. He was a strong advocate for a national museum, and chair of the relevant committee. In a room under the 'LegCo' building, Sir Allan introduced me to a newly-arrived Roy Mackay who was tending a small collection of artefacts. Roy had been recruited from the Australian Museum, Sydney, as director of the infant PNG counterpart. Although he had a role administering cultural property laws, Roy's main interest was in natural history. At the end of 1965, with Harry Bell, an Australian army officer serving with the Pacific Islands Regiment, he proposed establishing a New Guinea Bird Society. The nucleus of the membership was members of the Australian 'RAOU' (including me) who were contacted by reason of a Papua New Guinea address. I was a founding member and gave one of the early talks. Lady Cleland, wife of the administrator, and son Evan were early members.

I can put a date to these events by this report in the newsletter:

> The formation of the Society has been heralded by a note in the "South Pacific Post", an ABC interview given by Roy Mackay, and another on the Women's Session by Geoff Dabb. Following up this good publicity, the Museum has prepared a show-case dealing with the formation of the Society and its aims. Harry Bell, Hon. Secretary 18/12/65.

Once again, I was in the happy position of having the company of people who knew more about birds than I did, even if I had drawn ahead in the matter of accumulating bird books. Roy and Harry had had extensive experience in bird circles in Australia. Furthermore, reinforcements were gathering. Win Filewood, a biologist who lived in Papua New Guinea until December 1975, became the country's 'PJW' with regular articles in the *South Pacific Post*. A later useful contribution to the literature was *Birds of New Guinea and Tropical Australia* (1976) in which Win's text was combined with the remarkable photos of Bill Peckover. After that the bird literature for Papua New Guinea, as for other areas, benefitted (I suppose is the word) from a comparative explosion. Having mentioned useful books up to the mid-70s, I must draw attention to the informative 20 pages in the 'Birds' entry in

Encyclopaedia of Papua New Guinea, published in 1972. That was the work of Richard Schodde and Warren Hitchcock.

Today, the birds of New Guinea have been comprehensively covered in a continuing stream of books. Moreover, digital listing enables anyone interested to find recent records of a species, or records of the species seen at any particular place. I shall talk about that development in an appendix.

In late 1965, I met my future wife, although we were not married until end of 1968. Gretel, a few years younger than I was, had arrived from Sydney to stay with her older sister who was married to a kiap. A 'kiap' was an officer of the field staff who had the function of bringing orderly government to the people of the country. Gretel was taken down the Rigo Road to see the Osprey nest reported by Harry Bell, near Bootless Bay.

Roy Mackay was one of those complete field ornithologists, expert at identification by sight or call, and capable at things like mist-netting and banding. He had a keen sense of habitat and bird movements, as apparent from his Port Moresby book. He was a professional preparer of specimens. There was some collecting of specimens around Port Moresby. Roy had a short-barreled 12-gauge riot gun, with fine shot effective for the purpose. I sometimes accompanied him with my less-suitable gun, more useful for hunting ducks.

When Ian Rowley (CSIRO, Canberra) was doing his re-appraisal of Australian crows and ravens he wanted some crows from New Guinea. I had met Ian on a visit to Canberra, having driven to his Gungahlin office down the tree-lined avenue that led to the old building in those days. I volunteered to collect the crows, with Roy to process the skins. My chosen site was a garbage dump at Bomana Police College, where I had the help of a police officer. The Bomana locality, about 7 km from the airport, was the setting for the police college, the country's main prison, and the commemorative war cemetery. Unfortunately, most of my collected specimens turned out to be immatures. They are still in the CSIRO collection.

After 1967 for various reasons I went through a no-time-for-birds period, losing touch with the bird society, which was steadily gaining adherents. Many interesting things were going on in the government. The pace of social activity increased, perhaps to a reckless level. This might have contributed to the tuberculosis (both lungs), which entailed three months in Port Moresby hospital and two years of streptomycin injections. After recovery came a few years of competitive sailing on Port Moresby harbour, and a lot of general boating and fishing. The most enjoyable fishing required an early morning drive to float an aluminium dinghy (a 'tinnie' to Australians) in one of the tidal creeks that flowed into Galley Reach, an inlet 60 km north-west of Port Moresby. The fish-watcher was better served with books than the bird observer: Grant's *Guide to Fishes* (a Queensland publication, in various editions), and *The Fishes of New Guinea* by Ian Munro (1967). We caught Pikey Bream, Javelin Fish, Mangrove Jack and an occasional Barramundi.

There was also the matter of setting up in married housing. Over the next 11 years, we occupied three different houses in the town area, rather than in the expanding suburbs behind the hills, the first being on the edge of the sprawling complex of villages and settlements beside the harbour.

In 1970/71, we had a year in London where I was taking a master's degree. This time a pre-ordered vehicle was picked up in Rome. My travelling this time covered less ground than in 1965 with, in the circumstances, less serious searching for birds. I carried the revised edition of the same Peterson guide. As in the first edition, beneath the publishing history was the dedication, of a kind not unusual in bird books, 'To our long-suffering wives'. Beneath that, a literary allusion was added: '"She laments, sir … her husband goes a-birding." Shakespeare – *Merry Wives of Windsor.*'

One sighting from that year stays in the memory. In Italy, touring through the Abruzzi we came across the picturesque Lago di Scanno. A bare tree held a small group of unmistakable Purple Herons. I was delighted to find that the little Peterson guide denied the presence of that species in central Italy.

In the following years in Port Moresby, birds were not front of mind but never far away. A reason for that was that many people who visited New Guinea thought they would like to see some birds. They were probably vaguely thinking about birds of paradise. Various friends of mine would ask me to show their visitors 'some birds'. This was part of SHOWING VISITORS AROUND. The best places to go were Waigani Swamp and the adjoining sewage ponds, or Varirata National Park at the foot of the ranges. The lowland rainforest near or beyond Brown River was a possibility but in dense forest it is difficult to see birds. At some places you could expect to find Gaudichaud's Kingfisher, Orange-bellied Fruit-

Dove and a native starling or myna. A bird of paradise (*P. raggiana*) was possible early in the morning at the right place, in the Sogeri area. These days I think you would need to rely on a professional guiding service in visiting the same places.

One visitor was Sally, Duchess of Westminster, in her 60s and an adventurous traveller. She was quite interested in birds but more interested in sampling the crocodile-tail lunch that was sometimes on offer at the Rouna Hotel. The crocodile tails came from the farm at Moitaka that had pioneered breeding of the reptiles for their skins. On the day I went into the hotel to ask about that menu item, I had to report back that it was not available. Sally was not entirely satisfied. 'Did you tell them I'm a duchess?' she asked.

Varirata became a convenient venue to take official visitors who had a spare day in their program. About a year after independence, John Howard, a junior minister in the Fraser government, arrived with Mrs Howard. I think the occasion was the signing of a trade agreement. So, it was up to Varirata for them, as guests of the Papua New Guinea Department of Foreign Relations and Trade. I remember a pink-faced John Howard lying on his back under a tree fanning himself. He looked rather like John Denver in those days.

As I am about to move on to other matters, I mention here five fairly common bird species I associate with Port Moresby, although three are also on the Australian list. One is the Singing Starling. This smallish black bird seems more sleek and slender than the European Starling, with a bright red eye. It was a garden bird, sometimes seen feeding on the flesh of over-ripe bananas or papaya fruit. In the back-yard of one house we lived in, above Ela Beach, a flock would fly in to gulp down bird's eye chillies, quickly stripping a small bush. The colour of the chilli matched the eye of the bird. This suggested an origin of the name of the plant, perhaps referring to another red-eyed bird somewhere, although I have not read anywhere of that connection.

My second bird was also common, but easily overlooked. It was a small bird, the Rufous-banded Honeyeater *Conopophila albogularis*. These active little birds would hunt for caterpillars through the branches of the spreading Rain Tree just outside the bathroom window, so I could watch them some mornings while shaving. My third bird is a small grass-finch, the Grey-headed Mannikin, found in open spaces with short grass, like playing fields. Quite large flocks would silently gather to feed, coming down like a sudden shower of giant rain-drops.

My fourth bird, seen once, came from Australia, literally. Next to a house on the rocky hillside above the harbour there was just enough space for an above-ground pool. One morning, a guest gazing upwards while floating supine on an inflated mattress suddenly gasped 'What's *that*?!' 'That' was a large bird with a large bill perched near the top of a Terminalia ('beach almond') tree. It was a Channel-billed Cuckoo, evidently resting after a flight across the Coral Sea. It stayed in the same position for some hours, before resuming its travels.

My fifth bird is a common fairy-wren, found in the savannah where there is low shrubby growth or tangled high-grass. The male is black, with a small white crescent on the shoulder, a striking sight on my first encounter, not having known any fairy-wren in Australia other than the familiar 'Superb'. There is a poor picture of the New Guinea bird in Iredale. It is given better treatment in Richard Weatherly's *A Brush With Birds* (2020), where you meet it in his chapter on New Guinea. This endemic New Guinea species is now known as *Malurus alboscapulatus*, White-shouldered Fairy-wren – not so hard to find names for some new species, after all.

From Gould/Sharpe, *Birds of New Guinea and Adjacent Islands,* the Pied Maluris.

I had made some attempt to find out village names of some bird species. Conducted seriously, that project could take some time, given the number of species and the number of languages – more than 800, or 12% of the world total. (Curiously, the number of languages and the number of bird species, and their proportions of respective world totals, are quite similar, depending on the precise region adopted for the calculation.) I was told by a PNG lawyer from the Mekeo area that the Papuan Friarbird had a name that translated as 'village greeter'. I think you would find quite a few 'greeters', village and other, if you proceeded with that exercise.

Photo by Neil Murray in 1959, looking down
the Laloki Gorge from Rouna. At the far end
of the ridge on the right is Hombron Bluff,
from which you can see Port Moresby.
Below is Neil's photo of nearby Rouna Falls.
This was a well-known spot for watching
iridescent Glossy Swiftlets.

The Birds of New Guinea and the Adjacent Papua Islands was the last great work
assembled by John Gould, completed after his death, by Richard Bowdler Sharpe.
The illustrations below are of three species that can be found in forest areas of the
Port Moresby hinterland: Gaudichaud's Kingfisher, Raggiana Bird of Paradise, and
Magnificent Riflebird (as it was before recognised as a separate species).

About 1966, in the Law
Department at Konedobu.

1968 Taking a look at housing for the new
university in the Waigani valley. This was
on an afternoon's leave from hospital
during a period with tuberculosis.

December 1968. Wedding at a
church in Boroko
(Port Moresby suburb).

After the wedding, a few days at a
guest house at Tapini,
a government station.

Geoff Dabb wins Fireball medal

Geoff Dabb clinched the South Pacific Games yachting gold medal with a first and a second placing in the last two heats of the Fireballs sailed.

By discarding his worst heat of the seven sailed — his disqualification in the fifth heat where he lost 18 points — Dabb finished with only six points lost.

French Polynesian skipper Alan Burgaud, sailing Aureole, finished with the silver medal with 14.4 points lost overall.

Burgaud had won the sixth heat of the series and finished in third place in the seventh and final heat.

With 40 points lost, Fiji's Bill Gardiner just shaded team - mate Fred Reymond (44.1 points lost) to win the bronze medal.

The second French Polynesian, J. Arnould in Amanda Jane finished with 47.1 points lost to fill fifth place overall.

— Dick Jones.

The years before self-government. Right: *South Pacific Post* report of success at 1969 South Pacific Games on Port Moresby harbour, with help of expert crew, Greg Antonieff. Above: Who is this? Gerry Owers, whose name marks the southern end of the Kokoda Trail, was a surveyor at Wau in 1970. He drove me up to Edie Creek where he was surveying a mining lease. Below: In London, in December that year, the Alfa outside our house in a snowy Finchley. Two snaps below right: in Singapore on the way home. The famous Jurong Bird Park, now recently closed, had just been opened (in January 1971).

IV

Cassowaries (a digression)

I do not remember ever seeing a cassowary in the wild. In New Guinea you would sometimes see captive ones in various places. Sometimes I'd see them being transported in trucks, once even by air, in home-made crates. I was told by field officers on outstations that this was for bride-price exchange, but they are also used as food. They are often hunted. Once I took part in a prosecution that involved the shooting of a village woman who had been gathering bush food. She had been mistaken for a cassowary. Semi-tame birds in villages were reported to suddenly become aggressive, with an old person or a child sometimes falling victim to an attack with the powerful feet. There are occasional reports of assaults on tourists by Queensland cassowaries.

There are three species in New Guinea, one, the Southern Cassowary, *C. casuarius* being shared with north Queensland. That species, the largest of the three, also occurs in Indonesia on the Moluccan island of Seram (Ceram), where the species was first encountered by Europeans. Alfred Wallace later mentioned it in his *Malay Archipelago* (1869). The English and scientific names come from the Malay name *kesuar*.

There was no cassowary in Gould's *Birds of Australia*, the species not having been encountered there by Europeans by the publishing of the seventh volume (1848). In the *Handbook* (1865), Gould was able to report the probable existence of a cassowary in North Queensland, one having been shot by a member of the ill-fated Kennedy expedition (1848). 'The flesh was eaten and found to be delicious' (report in *Illustrated Sydney Herald* 3 June 1854.) The *Supplement* to *Birds of Australia* (1869) stated in the introduction: 'The most important addition to our knowledge of Australian Birds is the discovery of a fine species of Cassowary in the rich colony of Queensland …'

The Pidgin name for each of the three species is 'muruk' from the name in the Rabaul area for the smaller *C. bennetti* (Bennett's Cassowary, now more usually 'Dwarf Cassowary').

Bennett's Cassowary or Mooruk, from Gould's *Supplement to the Birds of Australia*

The name 'Bennett's Cassowary' comes from the naming of the species by John Gould for Dr George Bennett who had sent a live specimen to the Zoological Society in London. In his book, *Gatherings of a Naturalist in Australasia* (1860), Bennett includes a chapter, more than 20 pages, on *The Mooruk or Cassowary of New Britain, South Pacific Ocean (Casuarius bennetti)*. He describes how he kept a pair of these birds, brought down from the Rabaul area, at his house in Sydney.

> Having had these birds for a considerable time in my possession, I had ample opportunity of hearing all the notes uttered by them. I never heard them utter a sound like 'Mooruk'. I am inclined to consider the name signifies, in the native language, 'swift', resembling closely the Malay term '*a muck*'", or mad career; and the extraordinary rapid movements of these birds, which I shall have occasion to relate further on, rather confirm my idea on this subject.

(To explore this, I have consulted an online Kuanua / English dictionary, and can only find 'murup', which is given as the name of the cassowary. Unfortunately, I no longer have Tolai friends with whom I can take the matter further.)

Gould used the term 'Mooruk' for the smaller species, and 'the common Cassowary' or 'Australian Cassowary' for the larger one. 'Compared with the Cassowary, the Mooruk is a smaller and shorter bird and has much thicker legs …' (*Supplement*)

There is a useful account of the three species in *The Birds of Papua New Guinea* vol. 1 (1985) by Brian Coates. Another informative book is *Birds of My Kalam Country* (1977) by Ian Saem Majnep and Ralph Bulmer. This contains some 17 pages dealing with the Dwarf Cassowary, the main species found in the highlands. Saem talks about the cultural significance to his people of the *Kobty* to use the Kalam name. Bulmer adds comments from a different biological perspective. This is linked to a discussion of taxonomic classifications used by New Guinea peoples. Some regard the cassowary as in the same class as other birds; some regard it as a different kind of being from other birds. Bulmer had pointed out in an earlier paper how beliefs about the relationship between the cassowary and man gave rise to rules about how it should be hunted, and practices recognising its role in relation to two important foods, taro and pandanus nuts. The paper was titled, *Why is the Cassowary not a bird? A problem of zoological taxonomy among the Karam of the New Guinea highlands* (1967).

In writing this short note on the cassowary, I sought comments from Bryant Allen and Robin Hide, both former PNG (now Canberra) residents with a long academic interest in New Guinea. The latter drew my attention to his result of a quick online search of 'cassowary [titles only]'. This yielded 45 articles dealing with one or other aspect of the cassowary, bird or non-bird, most relating to New Guinea. Several articles relate to the important role of cassowaries of all three species in contributing to the health of the forests by spreading seeds.

I should add that in Ron May's guide to bush foods and the culinary arts of PNG (*Kaikai Aniani*, 1984), of possible bird food items, 'that which offers most as a table bird is the cassowary'. Sadly, no cassowary dish is included in the recipe section.

Above: a young Tony Siaguru, first head of PNG Foreign Affairs Dept, with Mina. Above right, at a Geneva Law of the Sea meeting, with Peter Donigi and Ben Sabumei. Right: The (earlier) 1974 Caracas Law of the Sea meeting, with Peter Donigi, Neroni Slade (Samoa) and David Tupou (Tonga). An 'Oceania Group' argued for full 200-mile zones for small islands.

Below: In 1974 as a prelude to formal agreement on the border with Indonesia, a week-long air trip along border stations was undertaken to inspect the markers that had been placed by survey teams.   Left , our aircraft at Tabubil, Hindenburg Wall in background. Centre, section of the unstable Fly River, forming part of the boundary. Right, boundary marker on the north coast.

Sunset, 15 September 1975: the Australian flag as the symbol of authority (right) is lowered for the last time. Over these few days Governor-General Kerr and Prince Charles, both visible in below snap, are reported to have discussed the approaching (Australian) constitutional crisis.

A more complex 'border' than people know, involving those northernTorres Strait islands, now important to birdwatchers. Left: A snap taken during negotiations, looking north over Boigu with the PNG coast beyond.

Right: Part of the 1873 nautical chart which showed that the line B marked the intended limits of Queensland jurisdiction over islands near Boigu, rather than line A, which had been assumed earlier to represent the 'border'.

Right: The territorial seas boundary between the two countries has been precisely drawn. The heavy line here shows the agreed boundary between Saibai and Dauan and the PNG mainland. Note extensive mangroves along PNG coast. The scale shows nautical miles. (1 nautical mile = 1.852 km)

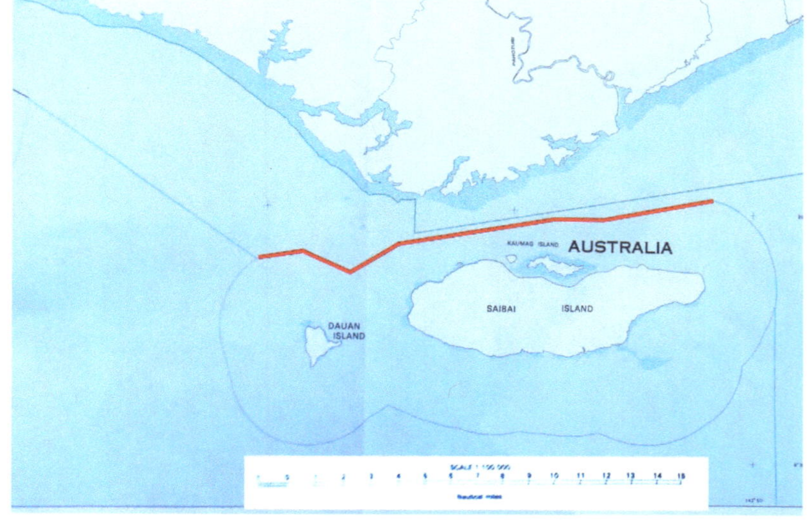

V

Later days in New Guinea;
national boundaries

Here I borrow my heading from the strongly opinionated Charles Monckton, who resigned from his post in British New Guinea in 1907, in disgust at the appointment by the new Australian administration of 'a lawyer as Governor, absolutely ignorant of anything to do with natives or the governance of a new country' (*Last Days in New Guinea*, 1922).

In my later years in Port Moresby, I was legal adviser to the recently-formed PNG Department of Foreign Relations and Trade. This involved work on treaties and new international arrangements. In view of the arrival of self-government (November 1973) and independence (September 1975), an important concern was sorting out national boundaries, and the related topic of the law of the sea. I need to say something about this, in view of the many months occupied by the Law of the Sea Conference, and, as we can now see, the implications of the new maritime zones for national bird lists.

That long process began in the United Nations General Assembly with debate about how to exploit the seabeds of the world's oceans. It was believed that vast resources existed in the form of mineral-rich potato-size 'nodules' that could be harvested only by the technically advanced countries. The subject of negotiation, then, was the seabed 'beyond national jurisdiction'. But what were the limits of national jurisdiction? At the time, extensive claims were being put forward, based on theories of an extensive 'continental shelf' or an asserted 'territorial sea' of comparable extent. The possible recognition of a wide territorial sea raised concerns about transit rights of commercial shipping – and transit for military purposes, for example by submarines and aircraft.

The essence of the bargain that emerged involved recognition of (a) a 12-nautical-mile territorial sea as an extension of the sovereignty of the coastal state; (b) a 200-nautical-mile 'exclusive economic zone' (EEZ) where the coastal state would control access to resources; (c) some extension of seabed control beyond 200 miles where justified by a broad continental shelf; (d) regimes of transit for ships and aircraft which varied according to whether the sea area was internal waters, territorial sea, or EEZ, (or within an international strait or within 'archipelagic waters').

As might be imagined, the details to fill out that basic scheme were quite complicated. Papua New Guinea had a particular interest in the questions (a) what small islands (perhaps really tiny uninhabited ones) might fail to qualify for an EEZ; (b) what arrangements would apply to managing so-called highly migratory species, like tuna, that moved across EEZs; (c) what rules would apply to setting boundaries between overlapping territorial seas and EEZs; (d) which sea areas would qualify as 'archipelagic waters'.

Over two years, preparatory meetings in New York and Geneva were held to set the scene for a major conference that would adopt a comprehensive treaty. This was to be in Santiago, Chile. However, that venue became unavailable after the coup that toppled the Allende government. Oil-rich Venezuela stepped in with an offer to host the conference at Caracas. The facility offered was a large hotel/apartment complex that was due to be opened in mid-1974. The date is easily fixed because the Nixon resignation occurred during my time at that conference session. During the critical week, the tension mounted each day as US delegates whispered in the corridors: 'We're told not to leave our television sets'.

There was to be no Treaty of Caracas. Opposing positions were aired, with no real progress towards compromise. Negotiations continued at sessions alternating between New York and Geneva, and, although the main elements were agreed by the end of 1977, the UN Convention on the Law of the Sea was not signed until December 1982.

I turn to the birds of Caracas. As you might have guessed, there was NO FIELD GUIDE, not that I could find at the time, anyway. The helpful Roger Tory Peterson had produced *A Field Guide to Mexican Birds and Adjacent Central America* (1973), which I picked up at the overnight stop in Mexico City. In the little shop in the Caracas complex, I found *A Guide to the Birds of South America* (1970) by Rodolphe de Schauensee ('130 Bs.' - referring here to the bolivar, as it was at that time). These were of limited help. Tantalisingly, the latter advertised on the dust jacket a guide to the 1556 birds of neighbouring Colombia, a book I could not find anywhere in Caracas. After leaving Caracas, I came across *Hundred of the Best Known Birds of Venezuela* (1953, 1963) by Kathleen D. Phelps. That would have been helpful, and even more so *A Guide to the Birds of Venezuela* by de Schauensee and W. Phelps Jr, but that did not appear until 1978.

I now read that the Phelps Ornithological Collection in Caracas contains 'probably the finest single-country collection of bird specimens in the world'. That is a description given in *Birds of Northern South America: An Identification Guide* (2006), by Robin Restall and others. That was a book far into the future.

In any case, I could only do some opportunistic bird observing. I easily picked up common birds like the Saffron Finch, Carib Grackle, Great Kiskadee, Tropical Mockingbird and Blue-grey Tanager, according to Kathleen Phelps 'one of the best known and loved birds of Venezuela'. There were some conspicuous green parrots. On a trip with a small party of fellow delegates to Lake Calabozo for piranha fishing, I had a close view of a beautiful little green and white swallow, perched on a stump just above the water. On a sight-seeing excursion with 'Bodo's Safaris' in a zebra-striped minibus we came across some forest birds including a puffbird and a jacamar. One weekend a local businessman took us on an overnight yacht trip of some 140 km to Islas Los Roques. In the morning, Brown Pelicans and Brown Boobies plunged into the sea by the gently rocking Columbia 50, as we lunched on the pickled squid provided by our generous host.

Pending a final treaty, the extension of sea jurisdiction possible under the emerging law of the sea made it necessary to attend to new boundaries. In due course, it also provided a basis for seaward limits for recording birds on national lists. The present Australian Rarities Committee accepts records of birds at sea 'within the exclusive economic zone'.

Back in New Guinea, a matter needing attention was the land boundary with Indonesia on the island of New Guinea. In 1974, Indonesia and Australia, with PNG agreement, confirmed the boundary set by the original colonial powers, United Kingdom, The Netherlands and Germany. One point at issue was of some importance to future bird-seeking tourists. In the south, the line of the border ran north from the mouth of the Bensbach River. Indonesia expressed the view that over 80 years, based on co-ordinates specified in 1894, the river mouth had moved some 1,200 metres to the west. Adopting those coordinates would have placed the river entrance entirely in Indonesia. Fortunately for the future of the Bensbach Lodge, that claim was dropped, after expert evidence was called on. The sea boundaries to the north and south were agreed by applying the equidistance rule.

The Torres Strait boundary was a much more complicated matter, with some implications for the Australian bird list. PNG ministers were unhappy about the Australian 'boundary' shown on maps as so far north that it seemed to run along the PNG coast. This was the result of a pre-emptive acquisition by Queensland of certain islands in colonial days, as a prelude to the annexation of British New Guinea. PNG ministers raised the matter before independence, and growing awareness of possible sea and seabed resources made it necessary for something to be done about it. The initial PNG request was, in effect, for transfer of the Australian islands in the northern part of Torres Strait. That was not going to happen. The islanders did not want it and Queensland did not want it. There was a constitutional bar to the transfer by the Commonwealth of any Queensland territory without Queensland consent.

High rainfall in the mountainous central region of New Guinea led to heavy discharge of sediment down the Fly River, which was pushed back against the coast by the prevailing south-easterlies, over time creating mud-banks and islands. Relatively large low islands were Daru (in PNG), and Saibai and Boigu (in Australia). During the negotiations, we flew low over the area in a helicopter, startling deer that fled splashing through the swamps, and great waterbirds that could be seen clearly in ponderous flight.

The arrangements that were finally agreed established sea and seabed boundaries that ran much further to the south than a median line between Australian islands and the PNG coast. However, Australian sovereignty over the islands was recognized, together with adjoining areas of territorial sea limited to three rather than the possible 12 miles. The treaty was signed on 18 December 1978. The negotiations had been quite difficult, even tense at times, involving ministers on both sides and a range of officials. As mementos for myself and Tony Siaguru (head of PNG foreign affairs), I asked Australian counterparts to get their ministers to sign souvenir copies of the treaty. I was told that a hesitant Andrew Peacock had asked, 'Are you sure that this isn't some kind of trick?' I still have my copy. Two Australian counterparts, Malcolm Lyon and Dick Smith, had their own copies signed by PNG ministers. Sadly, I have just realised that of the eight people most involved at the end, four politicians and four officials, I am the only one still with the living.

So, how close is Australia to Papua New Guinea? Pre-independence maps, for example the one accompanying the *Encyclopaedia of Papua and New Guinea* (1972), show Australian islands that are less than 1 km from the Papuan coast, and even closer at low tide. However, during negotiations it was recognized that, on a careful reading, three very close, uninhabited inshore islands had not been caught by the Queensland Coast Islands Act of 1879, so were part of PNG. Today the closest points of dry land are about 4 km apart. However, drying mudbanks, for example near Moimi Island (Australia) and Kussa Island (PNG), are much closer. Of course, the territorial seas of the two countries adjoin one another. Near neighbours indeed.

Some half-dozen bird species are on the Australian list by reason of their appearance at Boigu or Saibai Islands. No doubt the number would be increased by more systematic observing. One of these is the Singing Starling. According to the *Australian Bird Guide,* a small resident population colonised Boigu Island in the mid-1980s. This 'forages for fruit within gardens' – no surprise there. At the time of writing, a report of a Long-tailed Buzzard is 'under review'.

At the end of 1979, after 17 years, it was time to leave PNG. Although the work was rewarding, I was becoming uncomfortable as a white face at the upper levels of government advising. The shortage of capable Papua New Guineans in the government legal area was quickly being overcome. Two that I had been with at the Caracas conference achieved diplomatic prominence. Tony Siaguru became Deputy Secretary-General at the Commonwealth Secretariat in London. Peter Donigi, after a period in legal practice, returned to the diplomatic field and, in 2001, became president of the Assembly of the International Seabed Authority.

Another thing, social conditions were deteriorating. Of various possible courses, I decided to try government work in Canberra. I had been dealing with people there in various departments, and the life-style seemed likely to suit me, at my age of 42.

Soon after I became a Canberra resident, I was talking to an Australian trade official who knew of my interest in birds, and knew how colourful life could be in New Guinea. 'We're all brown sparrows down here, Geoff ', he said. And so we all were, in some ways.

VI

To Canberra

I've noticed that Australian government officials don't write much for public consumption about the work they do, or did. Perhaps the reason is that it would be fairly boring to the general public, or there is a concern about unauthorised disclosure. Nonetheless, I have something to say about the system of government in Australia. The central government is one of limited powers. However, there are some areas where the Commonwealth could take responsibility, but doesn't, because it doesn't want to, especially under parties of the Right. Sometimes it's a matter of the Commonwealth lacking the personnel or the practical means, as when it handed the territorial sea to the States to administer, under the so-described offshore constitutional settlement, in 1980. I have another example, and it concerns birds.

I was in part of the Attorney-General's Department that considered constitutional questions, particularly arrangements for giving effect to international treaties. In 1974, the Whitlam government had entered into a treaty with Japan to protect birds migrating between the two countries. The Commonwealth could have legislated for the necessary bird protection, and made arrangements for the States, if necessary, to help with enforcement. However, the Fraser government pursued a policy of 'cooperative federalism'. Under this, each Australian State and Territory would put in place laws protecting the relevant migratory birds, and give an assurance to the Commonwealth that the laws would be appropriately enforced. Certainly some kind of cooperation between jurisdictions was going to be needed, but the Commonwealth position then was that, treaty or no treaty, fauna protection was best treated as a State responsibility.

There was a problem. It had been established that, under the Constitution, State laws did not apply in places owned by the Commonwealth. That situation had been met by a Commonwealth law that applied State laws in Commonwealth places as if an ordinary part of the State. However, that arrangement was subject to the possibility of an applied State law being excluded by another Commonwealth law applying to the 'place'. Someone had pointed out that the relevant migratory birds were likely to be found in some 'Commonwealth places', for example airports or defence training areas, that were governed by specific Commonwealth rules. State bird-protection laws would not, or might not, apply there.

The result was that the migratory birds treaty could not be brought into force until arrangements were made to ensure that authorities administering Commonwealth-owned airports and defence areas, or other Commonwealth-owned areas, were instructed to adopt protective measures in relation to the listed bird species. The file was still in the pending tray when I arrived in Canberra – not that I can take much credit for advancing the matter. A change of government fixed that.

Another issue arose out of that 'cooperative federalism'. Maintaining that management of land was a State responsibility, the Fraser government had set itself against use of its 'external affairs' law-making power to over-ride State decisions in that area. Then the matter of the proposed Franklin Dam in Tasmania came along. Some people thought the Commonwealth should do something about that. A respected A-G's department lawyer, Dennis Rose, wrote an opinion arguing that a Commonwealth law stopping the dam would be justified, if not required, by Australia's obligations under the UNESCO World Heritage Convention. The Fraser government was not attracted to that idea. However, the Hawke government came to office in March 1983 with a commitment to stop the dam, and quickly obtained passage of the necessary legislation. The story of the Tasmanian Dam case, upholding that use of the external affairs power, has been told in other places. Thinking about it, I can point to no close connection between the Dam Case and birds. (Birds are likely to have more relevance to stopping windfarms.) However, I can think of one incident with a slight connection to wildlife.

Gareth Evans, the Attorney-General, was the minister with responsibility for stopping the dam. In setting up the detail of the legislation, it was convenient to use as a reference point a 'flying-fox pylon', part of an arrangement for crossing the river. On being briefed about this, Gareth Evans was puzzled by this expression, apparently hearing, as he grappled with the many other issues occupying him at the time, something like 'flying-fox pile-on'. After some further discussion, understanding dawned. 'Oh', he said, 'you mean this is a *man-made* structure!'

Here are some basic points about our living in Canberra. We had a house in the suburb of Chapman, and like many Canberrans acquired a coast house, this one at Tuross Head. We also acquired a daughter, initially named 'Sarah', but, when that name seemed to be so common it became confusing, it was changed to 'Serin', the name of a bird, taken from the Peterson field guide (the one for Europe, not Mexico). This was successful. There have been very few Serins about to cause confusion.

After being out of the country for 17 years, I needed to catch up with Australian birds. There had been a development, the appearance of 'field guides in the modern sense'. Artist Peter Slater had produced, separately, guides to 'Non-passerines' (1970) and 'Passerines' (1974). Graham Pizzey produced his first guide in 1980. My hard-cover copy of the latter has a price tag indicating its purchase at Dalton's, Canberra, after November 1980.

I won't recount all the relatively casual bird-observing that took place in those years. I remember the occasional Crescent Honeyeater in the garden at Chapman, and Lewin's Honeyeaters and curlews at the coast. Azure Kingfishers and Striated Herons could be seen in the low mangroves in the Tuross estuary. An occasional sighting of Crested Pigeons at Belconnen golf course foreshadowed the coming appearance of that now-common species throughout Canberra. As to travel, I made two trips back to PNG in connection with the Torres Strait Treaty. An interesting trip as regards acquisition of bird books was to Jamaica. This was in connection with the signing of the Law of the Sea Convention, in December 1982.

Jamaica had been confirmed as the site of the International Seabed Authority, which was to control mining in the seabed area beyond national jurisdiction. The venue for the signing was a location on the north coast near Montego Bay. It might have been offered because the resort industry in Jamaica was in a slump, and there were reported to be near-empty hotels along that once-popular north coast. The accommodation for most delegations, the Rose Hall Resort, was named for a nearby mansion of the plantation era. The High Commissioner was kind enough to entrust to me the weekly mail run over to Kingston, travelling by small aircraft. This allowed me to visit a couple of bookshops. Among my purchases were *Bird-watching in Jamaica* by May Jeffrey-Smith and *Birds of the West Indies* (4th ed.) by James Bond.

The last-named has some notoriety by reason of the name of the author. It has been suggested that the book was the 'likeliest inspiration' for the name of Ian Fleming's character (e.g. *Canberra Times* 27 June 1996). Actually, there is firm evidence. I have a book *Ian Fleming*

Introduces Jamaica (1965) in which he writes that all his Bond tales were written at his Jamaican house, on the north coast to the east of Montego Bay.

> Here is another Jamaican link. I was looking for a name for my hero … and I found it, on the cover of one of my Jamaican bibles *Birds of the West Indies* by James Bond, an ornithological classic. (Only a couple of weeks ago, I met him, the real James Bond, and Mrs Bond, for the first time. They arrived out of the blue and couldn't have been nicer about my theft of the family name. It helped at the customs, they said!)

Among remembered Jamaican birds were the ever-present Bananaquit, Blue Quit, Saffron Finch (introduced from South America, apparently), a hummingbird (Jamaican Mango, probably) at the nearby golf course, and a tropicbird beating against the north-east tradewind a little out from the shore.

In 1985, I went with the family on a posting to the Australian Embassy in Washington for three years.

VII

Washington DC

Among the books I brought with me was a copy, acquired and used in New York years before, of Roger Tory Peterson's *Field Guide to the Birds*. This was a revised edition of the original guide published in 1934, the model for the Europe guide I had used in 1965. By 1985, the Peterson guide was only one in a congested field of popular books about the bird life of North America. The second edition of the spectacular National Geographic *Field Guide to the Birds of North America* (1987) came out while I was there. I got my copy at National Geographic headquarters, just around the corner from the Australian Embassy.

The house we rented was just beyond the DC boundary but within the Beltway, in Maryland, in the Little Falls corner of Bethesda, between Mass. Avenue and the Potomac. It was a pleasant leafy area, good for suburban birds. We once had a Great Horned Owl in the garden.

An obvious difference from the Australian suburban bird scene was the woodpeckers. Within a couple of kilometres you could find six species, although you'd need to be lucky with the Red-headed. The smaller ones did a kind of noisy drumming. They were there year-round, even with heavy snow. In the backyard was a stand of tulip trees, *Liriodendron tulipifera*. One spring a pair of Northern Flickers (a woodpecker) dug a nest-hole in the soft wood. No sooner was it finished than a party of starlings appeared and one entered the hole. The male flicker dragged it out, only to have another one slip in. Eventually, the flickers gave up and moved away. Starlings had been pests in depriving Eastern Bluebirds of hollows, so you would see boxes that had been erected on posts, with holes large enough for bluebirds but not starlings. I'm told that proved to be a successful measure.

I joined the Audubon Society and attended meetings of the local 'chapter' at its headquarters in neighbouring Chevy Chase. There were two kinds of outings, some led by paid experts and some led by member volunteers. The paid ones were preceded by one or more evening meetings that explained what you were likely to see. One involved a shorebird expert, Claudia Wilds, author of *Finding Birds in the National Capital Area* (1983). Two lead-up meetings were held, one dealing with the sandpiper group and one with the plovers. The outing in a hired minibus was an all-day affair touring mud-flats around Delaware Bay. I particularly remember the Stilt Sandpiper. I also remember the excitement when a Red-necked Stint (a common bird as a migrant to Australia) was seen in a huge flock of other small sandpipers. One country's rarity can be a ho-hum bird in another. We also found an Upland Sandpiper at the expected spot, while peering through the fence at Dover Air Force Base. 'This is where they bring back the bodies', someone said.

Here are some other bird-observing moments. One Thanksgiving weekend we stayed at a beach house of friends at Bethany on Delaware Bay. I drove down to Chincoteague where they hold a waterfowl festival. It was a good place for one: there were great ponds covered with ducks and geese. I remember particularly the numbers of Snow Geese that had arrived from breeding grounds in the arctic tundra. Quite different incoming migrants were seen in New Mexico. At a crime prevention seminar at the university in Albuquerque, a local academic participant, Peter Lupsha, offered to show me something unusual. He drove me a distance of about 140 km to Bosque del Apache wildlife refuge where two Whooping Cranes were foraging in a flock of Sandhill Cranes. The smaller cranes had been used as foster parents in a recovery program.

Like other people in the embassy, for leave we took long driving holidays to traditionally recommended locations, for example the compulsory 'southern' trip. With the on-water excursion at Okefenokee Swamp came a knowledgeable guide. Among other things, he promised a 'Barn Owl', which was pointed out at its regular spot. We had an argument, raising voices from opposite ends of the boat. 'Excuse me, that's not a Barn Owl', I said. 'That *is* a Barn Owl, sir', and so on. It turned out it was a Barred Owl, the rhotic accent of the guide pronouncing the 'r' and not the 'd'. On the same trip, the Everglades were disappointing, I thought, but Sanibel Island made up for it. There were easy views of Roseate Spoonbill, Wood Stork, Tricolored Heron, Reddish Egret, both pelicans and several raptors. Incidentally the Osprey is a common and conspicuous species along much of the indented Atlantic coast of the US, with active nest platforms separated by only a few hundred metres in some places.

I went to see the counters in action at Hawk Mountain, Pennsylvania. From the information centre this was a short walk up a hill to the summit, where a group of mainly youngish people sat around on the rocks with binoculars. Some were holding large clip-boards, and saying things like 'Sharp-shin at 4 o'clock'. At this point, I must explain that my bird-observing in the USA was not really an aimless pastime. I brought a background as a consumer of books. For many years I'd had a copy of Peterson's *Bird Watcher's Anthology* (1957), a compilation of 85 essays or extracts from a wide range of writers about birds and the observing of them. One extract was entitled *Red-letter Day on Hawk Mountain*, by a curator at the site who 'had seen more hawks than any other living man'. It described a day when more than 7,000 migrating Broad-winged Hawks passed by in a single hour. In another book, *Birds Over America* (1948, paperback 1983), Peterson writes about birds and bird places. He gives his own account of Hawk Mountain, its huge numbers of passing hawks, and the crowds of watchers who go there. Hawk Mountain was just one place where the books I had read called for a visit.

Watchers on Hawk Mountain, Pennsylvania, Fall 1987.
The small person in the foreground is not actually watching.

Perhaps I should add at this point that I did have quite a busy working life at the embassy. This entailed liaising with the US Department of Justice and other agencies, reporting on aspects of the US legal system, dealing with private attorneys on legal matters, and some UN conference work in New York and Vienna.

Now I come to the warblers. Although there are other, unrelated, 'warblers' found in other places, these are the 'Wood Warblers' of the New World, a family of strongly migratory habits. More than 50 species come north of the Mexico boundary, some quite colourful and strongly marked when in breeding plumage. They travel north in spring, feeding on forest caterpillars that in turn feed on new green leaves. My first one was seen through the family room window feeding on caterpillars in a Pin Oak street tree. My Peterson guide told me that this was a 'Yellow-rumped ("Myrtle") Warbler'. Confusingly, it is regarded as a subspecies of a species that has a 'western form ("Audubon's" Warbler)'.

Although other species come with them, Peterson points out that people 'speak of the tides of birds that flood the countryside on certain days in May as *warbler waves*'. He says: 'If it were not for the warblers, birding would lose half its fun – in the East, anyway'. The local Audubon chapter called in two experts to lead a spring warbler 'foray' along the canal towpath by the Potomac. At the preliminary talk they showed pictures and played calls. I remember the call of the distinctive yellow Prothonotary Warbler. 'If we don't find this one, I'll resign', said one expert. He didn't need to. We found that one, and quite a few others. Most of them were named for colours, 'Prothonotary' referring to the yellow robes of certain church officials, and 'Cerulean' to the blue of the sky.

One Sunday, I took part in an annual bird count organized by the Audubon Society. The site to which I was assigned was the National Arboretum. There were only three other people including our leader and his wife. Our leader had a superb ear for calls, but had difficulty seeing birds. We had particular difficulty with a bird partly obscured by tree branches that was not calling. I could see it, as could the fourth member, but we did not know what it was. Our leader was becoming quite frustrated with our unhelpful efforts to describe it to him. It turned out to be an immature Orchard Oriole in an intermediate mottled plumage.

Washington years, 1985-1988.
The house in leafy Corewood Lane, Bethesda, Maryland.
You could identify the three common bird species from a modern field guide or from a volume of Audubon prints (upper row) or from the remarkable Frank Chapman & Chester Reed 'Color Key' published in 1903. In their book, the 'Northern Flicker' 412a is among the Woodpeckers, the 'Carolina Wren' 718 among 'Perching birds chiefly brown or streaked', and the 'Myrtle Warbler' 655 among 'Perching birds marked with yellow or orange'. Each species was also listed in a taxonomic table.

Return to Madang for a conference, 1999. View of sunrise from the hotel; flying fox design on souvenir shirt; some of abundant flying foxes at rest; tame kokomo (hornbill) kept at hotel.

Bustards I have known. Two snaps from Amby, Queensland, one from breeding program, at Serendip, near Geelong. Distant view of Great Bustards, Burgenland, Austria. Birdwatching Swedish delegate taking time from a Vienna conference on organized crime.

VIII

Canberra again

Back in Canberra in July 1988, there was a new parliament house, and a new public service. The long-standing view that the Australian Constitution required one department per minister, and vice versa, had been abandoned. The number of departments had been halved, with, as one example, the department dealing with policing and other law enforcement being rolled into the Attorney-General's Department. There was a more bureaucratic feel to the workplace, which was tending to be peopled by public servants rather than lawyers. Lawyers have, at least to some extent, an interest in the law; public servants have an interest in getting on in the public service.

Once more, I needed to think about where I was going. I was 50, and beginning to experience a twinge of irritation when working with people younger than myself, whose main interest was, well, getting on in the public service. I became more conscious of an obsession with hierarchy, going beyond a rational ordering of responsibilities. I had previously thought of higher-ups in the system, and even ministers, as, at least potential, friends. Two ministers in the Fraser government, Ian Macphee and Fred Chaney, had been close colleagues in New Guinea. A Hawke minister, Brian Howe, had been in the same year at Queen's College, where he was a rather uncommitted theological student. I had known Hawke during his time in Port Moresby as an industrial advocate on loan for a major case. Unintentionally, I had broken a bone in his hand with a long-necked Riesling bottle, carelessly wielded when we were trying to stop a dog fight at a party at his house in Chester Street (1966 that was, I think). I even had a slight connection with Barry Jones, having partnered him in the floral dance at the inaugural (and probably only) meeting of the Queen's College Cornwall Society. However, considering my options, I had decided not to look for a position overseas. I was not attracted to taking up private legal practice at that time. My background was in public, or 'government', law, and I knew that making a success of life as a barrister would involve long work hours, over evenings and weekends.

In deciding to accept a continuing life in the Australian public service, I had the prospect of a comfortable family life in Canberra, and some prospect of interesting work, meanwhile pursuing personal interests, including in the bird direction. Another consideration was that at the time the Attorney-General's Department was under amiable management, with Pat Brazil as Secretary and Lionel Bowen as Attorney-General. All that is by way of explaining how I came to spend the next 14 years engaged in government work, chiefly, if I had to summarise it, on legal aspects of the criminal justice system, law enforcement, and, later, national security issues. This was policy work. The department did not have an operational role in any of that, except in handling extradition requests and other formal requests for international assistance.

With pleasant memories of the Audubon chapter in Washington, I joined the Canberra Ornithologists Group, known as 'COG'. This was, and is, a happily diverse group, with 'professional ornithologists' from CSIRO and ANU, and other keen and experienced bird people, and a regular intake of beginner enthusiasts, many but not all drawn from the ranks of the retired. COG has monthly meetings, talks, regular local walks and longer outings, a newsletter and a quarterly journal. An early talk I offered was on 'Ospreys', drawing on my experience of that species around Washington DC. A more ambitious talk, lavishly illustrated, was on 'Field Guides of the World'. That was in a lecture theatre at Australian National University. The slide projector broke down during that one, on a subject difficult to present without pictures.

From COG members I have learnt a lot about the occurrence of birds around Canberra. The cumulative store of knowledge, some of it available in the Annual Bird Reports, some on a website, answers questions about local birdlife you could not answer by personal observing alone. Some members had much sharper identifying skills than mine, especially as regards calls. There were many opportunities to meet and talk to people who knew more about local birds than I did (although I had more bird books).

We moved to a house in a corner of Narrabundah where the streets are named for explorers. The address was (and is) on Brockman Street, which runs between Carnegie Crescent and La Perouse Street. Frederick Slade Brockman explored the Kimberleys in the early 1900s. David Carnegie also explored in Western Australia. After that he held a government post in Nigeria where he was shot with a poisoned arrow and died at the age of 29. Jean-Francois La Perouse was a famous French explorer who perished when his ship was wrecked on reefs in the Pacific in 1788. If you were an explorer today, you might feel a twinge of foreboding when standing at the intersection of Carnegie and La Perouse.

That intersection is also notable for being within a traffic warning area for peafowl. There is a long story behind the gathering in Canberra suburbs of these spectacular birds. They were drawn from farmlets adjacent to the suburbs by the braying of one particular pioneering peacock. Some other cities now have an urban peafowl problem, and complaints about our aggregation, now approaching a hundred-strong, nearly led to their removal. However, Canberra being Canberra, the Territory government decided protection rather than extermination would be the more enlightened course. Hence, we now have signs saying 'Wildlife Crossing. Peafowl' at each of the four approaches to the mentioned intersection.

When people say there are a lot of birds in Canberra they are usually thinking of the parrots and cockatoos. These are conspicuous and colorful birds. There are 23 species of parrots and cockatoos on the ACT bird list, but only 12 occur here regularly. Thirty years ago, two now-common species were not regarded as belonging to the Canberra area. These are the Little Corella and the Rainbow Lorikeet. In 1989, I noticed Little Corellas commuting over Narrabundah and tracked them to a rural lease known as 'Callum Brae' on Mugga Lane, where I found them nesting. There is still some uncertainty about whether our considerable numbers of those two species originated as escapes or releases or arrived here as part of a natural expansion. Having introduced myself to the Callum Brae owners, I was able to make regular visits there to look for birds. It is now a nature reserve.

Further afield, an advantage of participating in COG activities was the possibility of organised trips to new places. Sometimes these involved camping for a night or two, maybe three. Sometimes it was a coastal site, for example somewhere between Eden and Green Cape, or in east Gippsland, or the Shoalhaven area. More interesting to me were visits to the Mallee country, for example Round Hill or Yathong nature reserves, or to former sheep properties like Willandra, beyond Hillston, or Oolambeyan, near Hay. The latter was a NSW National Park, having been acquired as prime habitat for the Plains Wanderer. Sometimes the venue was a private property, a useful refuge from the camping crowds at Easter. Once the welcome at a property near Tullamore was so generous that I came away with two Muscovy Ducks in the car fridge, cleaned and plucked. This had slightly helped reduce the overpopulation of large, heavy free-range males, so aggressive that they were physically harming the much smaller females.

Some COG members had been pushing further afield, to build up their 'lists'. Typically undertaken by couples, a well-equipped sortie in a suitable vehicle could explore anywhere in Australia, the distance travelled depending only on the time available. For myself, a long single-purpose bird-focussed trip was not feasible or, at the time, appealing. However, it was quite feasible to combine bird-seeing with visits to family and friends. Gretel had a sister (still married to a kiap, although a different one) on an avocado farm between Ballina and Lismore. There was a niece near Lightning Ridge. I still had relatives in Geelong. We had good friends at Maleny (Sunshine Coast hinterland), and near the Daintree, in a home they had built next to the rain forest.

I have friends who have seen many more Australian bird species than I have. This is because they have systematically expanded their lists in the most bird-rich parts of the country. Not only do I fail to keep lists, but I have blanks as regards the birds of Western Australia and Tasmania. I did make a list of the birds around Broome on a short visit there to brief a new minister in the Howard government, on law enforcement matters. I remember being puzzled by a flock of what seemed to be unusual boobook owls. They were Little Corellas, thickly coated with the red dust of the arid zone.

Australia changed its extradition laws to make it easier to have treaties with countries that have different legal systems. In addition, a new kind of treaty was being developed to help in collecting evidence across international boundaries. There was a lot of travel in the course of this treaty work, usually on such a brisk schedule there was no time for birds. However, I found a little spare time in the course of a visit to South Africa. Apart from the wild birds, the museum in Pretoria was a revelation. As the owner of three different editions of *Roberts' Birds of Southern Africa*, I was impressed to enter the Austin Roberts Bird Hall and find a display of more than 800 species, all mounted, numbered and arranged in the order as in the book. 'We've got nothing like that in Canberra', I told them.

On a visit to London to negotiate an arrangement with the UK Home Office, I wandered into a small bookshop in search of bird books. The manager must have been an office-bearer of the Oriental Bird Club, because I came away signed up as a member. For several years after that I received a stream of copies of *Forktail* and other OBC publications, until I decided, with some regret, that this had to stop somewhere.

There was a visit to Madang, in connection with a gathering of government lawyers from around the Pacific. The accommodation was greatly improved from what I experienced on my first visit in 1962. In a nostalgic few hours I walked around and saw a few common birds. The town had become infested with great numbers of flying foxes, earning the status of unofficial town emblem. I supposed this was due to logging of the rainforest. Tim Flannery in *Mammals of New Guinea* (1990) assigns this population to Greater Flying Fox *P. neohibernicus*. In a subsequent edition (1995) this is corrected to Spectacled Flying Fox *P. conspicillatus*.

For various purposes, I made several visits to Vienna. The UN headquarters there was the home of a body that, under changing names, promoted cooperation on drug control and criminal justice matters. It was easy to explore the countryside by the excellent train system, being wary, of course, of the encephalitic ticks. At one series of meetings, I formed a friendship with a Swedish delegate who was familiar with European birds. He suggested a visit one weekend to see Great Bustards, in the Burgenland near the Hungarian border. With his scope, we did manage reasonable views, as well as seeing many other local species. At a gate onto a footbridge over a canal, I made to follow my companion, but he raised a forbidding hand. 'No', he said, 'I can go here as a citizen of the European Union' – meaning that I couldn't. This was the actual border.

For the next conference session we planned another visit, for which I needed to obtain a Hungarian visa. I hired a small car, and we set off on a Friday evening, reaching accommodation in Hungary that night. Over two days we covered a lot of ground at wetlands, fields and woods. An advantage was that most species were in full breeding plumage, particularly the shorebirds, and most particularly the variable Ruffs. There were a lot of ducks. The contrasting flashing wings of the White-winged Black Terns were a sight you would be unlikely to experience in Australia.

The contentious matter of the suburban peafowl. Above, a view from our bedroom window. Left, an unusual traffic sign, peafowl added. The white peahen survived for two years but was killed by a fox.. Below, new arrivals, one the white chick, call at the door of a neighbour.

IX

Pursuit of the image (1)

I am now going to talk about videoing and photographing. This requires some reference to the different ways people are becoming interested in birds. There is a question how to describe bird-interested people. In the 1950s, R.T. Peterson had written: 'Bird listing, or just plain "birding", not to be confused with serious bird watching, is basically a sport rather than a science.' When he said 'bird listing' or 'birding', Peterson was referring to the keeping of lists as a personal challenge, the aim being a long list, for whatever satisfaction that might bring. Peterson and other 'serious birdwatchers' did this as a side interest.

Sometimes 'birding' means birdwatching; sometimes it denotes something more competitive. As to which describes the more *serious* activity, we are on shifting sands. 'No longer is it accurate to call me a birdwatcher, a term the pros use to dismiss the spinsters and retired British army colonels who wait passively for birds to come to them. I have become an enthusiast, a chaser – a birder' (Mark Obasmascik, *The Big Year* (2004).) There is more discussion about this in Mark Cocker's *Birders: Tales of a Tribe* (2001). He refers to the eight sub-clans in the tribe, from 'scientist', through 'birder' and 'twitcher', to 'robin stroker'. Anyone interested in what serious birding is should take a look at the aims, activities and rules of the American Birding Association.

Along comes the new bird photography, now made much easier by the digital camera. Are people 'birdwatchers' if mainly interested in photographing birds? Clearly, they are not necessarily 'birders' in the competitive sense. However, there are different kinds of bird photography. Some people do it as a supplement to 'birding' or to 'serious birdwatching'. Some people pursue it as an end in itself, perhaps not much caring which species of bird it is. Some people do it for profit, and some do it competitively.

All the people referred to so far have some kind of interest in birds. The term 'bird-watcher' is not always appropriate, and 'ornithologist' is not suitable for most amateurs. We need a new, comprehensive term. I suggest they are all 'birdians'. After all, 'birdian' is no more unreasonable than calling a person interested in Doctor Who a 'whovian'. I shall leave the thought there. (On second thought, 'birdist' might be better. I am sure there is such a thing as 'birdism'.)

I had thought for a long time, since school days in fact, that serious bird photography involved too much effort and too much special equipment. I became mildly interested in image-capture with the 1980s generation of small video-cameras. These were compact and user-friendly and offered a fair degree of 'magnification' with the built-in 'zoom' capability. I experimented seriously with one in about 1990. It was not much good with small or distant birds. I still have some of that unsatisfactory footage, including, for example, quite a bit of the birds around the Daintree. Also, some of dense flocks of Budgerigars, swirling like clouds of green smoke over fields near Moree. I have some of various COG outings, and some I used at a recent talk on the Regent Honeyeater. That was taken at a banding operation in 1995 when four pairs were found breeding at North Watson in the north of Canberra.

I moved to still photography, which was still in the pre-digital era. After experimenting with a film camera attached to a telescope, I acquired a set of Canon lenses, second-hand and manually focussing. One was a 500mm, another 400mm, but allowing a large aperture of $f2.8$ and therefore constructed around a massive piece of glass and much heavier than the 500mm. This should be in a museum. Today's digital snappers might not know that you had a choice of negative film, for prints, or positive film that produced slides for use in a projector. I accumulated a large collection of slides, nearly all of low to medium quality. I learnt the limitations of manual focusing.

I took quite a few photos, though not mainly of birds, at the 2000 Sydney Olympics. There is a story behind that. In the planning for the Olympics it was considered that in the unlikely event of a terrorist incident it might be necessary to deploy the Defence Force. In theory, the army could be given a law enforcement role under an archaic procedure that left some doubt about use of powers when acting in support of State agencies. Accordingly, a new statutory procedure was put in place that would provide the necessary clarification, but at the price of rather complicated conditions that had to be satisfied before 'call out'. This meant that provision had to be made for legal advice along the way, so I was posted to Sydney for the duration of the games. As we all know, the Sydney Olympics were a great success, and, by good fortune, free of any serious unpleasantness.

My older sister was part of a partnership that owned a cattle property in Queensland. This was named 'Amby', and was south of the hamlet of that name, near Mitchell. The Maranoa River was nearby. I made three or four visits there to look into the birdlife, which included bustards and brolgas. After one stay there, I took an indirect route back to Canberra, travelling west through Charleville and Quilpie, as far as Noccundra, where I turned back east. Near Thargomindah, I had a memorable bird encounter. I collided with an emu. One moment it was quietly feeding some distance from the road, before suddenly dashing into the path of the vehicle, which, incidentally, was not mine but the subject of government hire for my use. After that I decided I needed a couple of quiet days camping, so I headed for a turn-off at Lake Bindegolly that I had used as a roadside stop on previous occasions. I found two other people there, obviously photographers, from their camera gear. One of these was Graeme Chapman, well-known ex-CSIRO photographer, with another professional photographer who was picking up hints in handling bird subjects. I spent the next couple of days with them.

I was interested in their views on new camera equipment. They were impressed by a new Canon digital camcorder, the XL1, which could use interchangeable Canon lenses, with a 7x 'magnification factor' due to the small sensor. This meant that an image taken with a 300 mm lens would crop to the equivalent of 42x magnification, so that a small bird at an approachable distance could more than fill the screen. For bird photographers, the pursuit of 'magnification' to the neglect of clarity is an urge that needs to be kept under control. However, the illusion of magnification via a small sensor seemed attractive in those early digital days. Graeme spoke glowingly of the possibilities of video in capturing bird behaviour. I decided to go down that road.

At Lake Bindegolly, I recorded a few species for the then current RAOU Atlas project, including a colony of nesting Caspian Terns on an island in the lake. At Cunnamulla, I checked into the police station in case I needed to report the matter of the emu. The officer had no interest in such a commonplace incident until he was struck by the thought that I might be covering up a more serious kind of accident, so we went outside to have a look. 'Yes', he said, 'I can see that you have definitely struck an animal of some kind'. I can put a date to those events. After a night in a Nyngan motel, I turned on the television and found a different world. It was 11 September 2001 in New York. The next few weeks were quite busy in my part of the Attorney-General's Department.

Contrasting scenes. Sydney 2000 - the bridge from Blues Point, and the crowd on the Domain from the Macquarie Street office. Gulls wait for chips, Sydney Fish Market.

Graeme Chapman and Andrew Tatnell, Lake Bindegolly, Queensland, September 2001.

A bird-banding team relaxes in the heat of the day beneath a Kurrajong tree. The Weddin Mountains, really just hills, are behind.

Weighing, measuring and photographing. The two-person team on the right is working with a Diamond Firetail, a bird too small to appear in any detail in this photo.

A Black-chinned Honeyeater shows its new band, and a Crested Shrike-tit tries to attract the attention of a bander.. These birds can give quite a sharp nip.

X

Pursuit of the image (2)

I ceased full-time work at the beginning of 2002, at age 63. I acquired the Toyota Prado and a suite of camping gear, far too much of it. Also the Canon XL1 and a set of lenses that would extend its reach. This recorded to mini-DV cassettes. I never re-used a cassette, so acquired a great number of full, unedited cassettes with a lot of rubbish in between useable footage of birds.

Any amateur accumulator of video or photos of birds comes up against the question: what do you do with the end-product? One answer, perhaps not entirely satisfying, is that you don't need to do anything with it. However, I joined the local video club, as a way of learning about video techniques. I began producing edited videos about bird subjects, recorded on DVDs. I would add a voice commentary. A few of these, I like to think, will have some historic interest. The problem with this activity is that you get overtaken by the technology. Mini-DV did not have enough pixels to meet what is now regarded as an acceptable 'high-definition' standard. You could not extract from a frame a still image that would meet exacting publishing requirements. The DVDs still make interesting viewing. I included a lot of copyright and performance-protected music, relying on a licensing arrangement through the video club, but I am not confident of the extent of that authorisation for a public airing today of my little compositions.

To give an idea of what I was about over that period, I mention the following titles:

Child of Sound - The name referred to one rendering of Gould's name 'Gerygone'. It was about the White-throated Gerygones nesting in Canberra woodlands. *The Last National Waterbird Championships* - This was about an imaginary sporting event, and won a national video competition. *Two Endangered Species*, admittedly not an inspired title, was about appearances of Regent Honeyeater and Swift Parrot in the Canberra area.

A Canberra Birdwatcher's Queensland Diary recorded encounters with north Queensland species, some from around the Daintree and Julatten. It included a Golden Bowerbird at Paluma, where *Triflebird* (can you guess the species?) was also filmed (at the trifle-dispensing tea-house). While at Paluma I came across Roy Mackay, from New Guinea days. He was living in the former Frith house. (I have recently learnt that Paluma lost Roy a year or so later. He had been a valued member of that community since ending his service at Baiyer River in the New Guinea highlands.)

Gavan Grassbird and the Waders included footage of Pectoral Sandpiper and Long-toed Stint together in Canberra. Another local wetlands production was ***Snipe Summer***. ***Gluepot*** was a record of a visit to that nature reserve in 2003, when the information centre was being set up. I came across Graeme Chapman there with Pam, photographing hybrid Black-eared Miners. I was able to catch photographer and bird on video.

The Honeyeater and the Mistletoe was about Painted Honeyeaters, in particular in Binya State Forest near Griffith. I was fortunate to meet a research student there undertaking his doctoral work on the species.

I spent some time on ***Looking for Spotty***. This began with a book known from childhood, *Spotty the Bowerbird and other Nature Stories* (E. S. Sorenson, 1920). The video showed the little book in the 'rare book' holdings of the National Library, followed by illustrations, again in the NLA, of the species in the Gould and Mathews volumes. Then there was an interview with Dick Schodde, holding specimens and discussing the bird, in the wildlife collection at Gungahlin. Spotted Bowerbirds in the wild were shown, where I had met them at Belyando, Eulo and Bowra (all Queensland) and then at Round Hill nature reserve. I made a separate video about ***Bowra***, which I visited three times when it belonged to the McLarens. Bowra was not far from the haunt of the original Spotty, by the Warrego River. There had been a Spotty bower in Julie's garden. The story ended with a preview of Peter Marsack's cover for the forthcoming HANZAB volume 7, where Spotty had been overlooked in favour of the similar Western Bowerbird.

Photographing Wildlife in Central Australia was a longer video, being a record of a visit to Uluru, where Adam Leavesley was doing work for his Ph.D. comparing bird communities in burnt Mulga at various stages of regrowth. We were able to camp in the actual Mulga around Uluru. This production was sent to a video club in the UK, to give them an idea of what we were videoing in Australia (more or less).

O is for Oolambeyan combined footage from two visits, in 2006 and 2007. I was able to include some Plains Wanderer and Australian Pratincole and, unusually, outside but near the national park a pair of Oriental Plovers. Another video, ***Nocoleche***, was about a reserved area not usually open to the public, south of Wanaaring, on the Paroo. Other western NSW DVDs were records of COG visits to Yathong and Round Hill reserves.

Last Spring at East O'Malley took several weeks to compile. It was a record of nesting birds at a woodland site near a Canberra suburb. The problem was that the woodland was about to be replaced by more suburb. The nesting birds included Little Eagle and Varied Sittella. As an example of what you can come across by way of action, a sequence of an Eastern Brown Snake taking a Double-barred Finch from a nest was included as a separate item.

Visits to the Western Treatment Plant in Victoria, usually referred to as 'Werribee', led to a video named, rather unimaginatively, ***Wetland***. This was more or less my home area. I could remember when the Melbourne-Geelong road was entirely one-lane, not even by-passing the town of Werribee. We small children had turned out to wave flags when the Governor-General, the Duke of Gloucester, with the Duchess of Gloucester, drove by along the Melbourne Road. A few years later we cheered again, as older children, when fellow schoolboys took part in the torch relay along that road, for the Melbourne Olympics in 1956. My Werribee video was able to include footage of quite a few species, including an unlikely Red-necked Phalarope in breeding plumage.

I had made a point of collecting footage of Swift Parrots on their occasional transits through Canberra, beginning with an occasion when they could be seen very close-up in flowering gums in the suburb of Cook. In May 2007, I was asked by the recovery program to visit Kurri Kurri, near Cessnock, where a parrot breeder, Greg Masters, had succeeded in breeding Swifties in captivity. The idea was to get video of caged birds at or in tree hollows, as an alternative to visiting the breeding haunts in Tasmania. As it happened, the birds at the time had no interest in hollows, so no success there. I was able to get some footage of wild parrots in angophora at Bateau Bay. With that, and material from elsewhere, I was able to deliver some footage for the program's education purposes.

A group of retired biologists had formed a team with a long-running interest in ***Montague Island***, a nature reserve, near Narooma, NSW south coast. As a volunteer project, they surveyed the wildlife there in cooperation with the NSW Parks service, with a particular focus on the nesting colonies of shearwaters. With respect to nesting ranges, the island was at the southern limit for the Wedge-tailed, and the northern limit for the Short-tailed. A significant anniversary of the surveys was coming up, so Chris Davey and Peter Fullagar asked me to come down to make a video record of the occasion. As usual, accommodation was in the staff quarters attached to the lighthouse. A first visit was in October 2008. A second visit in March 2009, when shearwater chicks were extracted from burrows, weighed and banded, marked the 50th year of this remarkable project. I produced a 70-minute package of video material.

A 10-minute segment was devoted to the arrival by helicopter of an ABC team with Geoff Sims, to make a report about the survey for national television. My own segment, which included Geoff interviewing Peter Fullagar while holding a squirming shearwater nestling, was longer than what was shown on television. And more interesting, I thought. Our party's stay on the island was extended for several days because the boat that was to take us off was prevented by weather from crossing the bar at Narooma. We were beginning to see the bare lining at the base of the freezer that held our food stocks.

I had enjoyed composing videos, a time-consuming hobby, suitable for a retired person. However, after some eight or nine years of videoing activity, my equipment had been superseded. My 'Casablanca' editing system, which was dedicated to video, was not able to handle large amounts of pixels. I reverted, with new equipment, to still photography, which was more useful for some purposes, such as getting images for talks. Furthermore, I had found that people were often looking for good still images of a species for a particular purpose.

Montague Island
Shearwater Project;
visit of ABC news
team, March 2009

A periodic visit to the Werribee area. 1. - An explosive take-off by sandpipers near the boat ramp. 2. - A patrolling Spotted Harrier. This is a favourite spot for the two harriers and other raptors. 3. - Hundreds of Pink-eared Ducks rise from Lake Borrie, You Yangs in background. 4.- Red-necked Phalarope and friends.   5.- Banded Stilt and Avocet in saline pond at Avalon.

XI

Pursuit of the image (3), and related projects

An example of a specific use was, with Jerry Olsen, reading the band of a long-lost Southern Boobook on Black Mountain (really just a hill, in the centre of Canberra). Later, Black Mountain was the subject of my talk about the birds that could be found there over the years. Unfortunately, the expansion of adjacent roads and hazard-reduction burning have reduced the birdlife, although the well-watered botanic gardens (ANBG) remain a popular bird-observing venue in winter.

An overview of what can be found in that nature reserve has been provided in *Black Mountain – a natural history of a Canberra icon* (2020), by Ian Fraser and Rosemary Purdie. That book is a follow-up to a symposium held in August 2018 to mark the 50th anniversary of declaration of Black Mountain as a park for conservation purposes. A program of informative walks was organized for the next day. I led one to look for birds. On the day, people looking at trees, flowers and rocks would have had much more luck. For birds, it was wrong time of year, wrong time of day. I would have liked to slip over the fence into the botanic gardens to look for a Bassian Thrush or Rose Robin.

For the Black Mountain talk I could draw on three earlier studies. One was by Harry Bell, who after leaving PNG in 1978 had gained his doctorate for work on thornbills, and made a study of the effect of a powerline clearing on Black Mountain. A second was by Stephen Marchant, later prominent in national bird circles, who over four years (1964–1968) had surveyed birds on the western slopes, towards what is now the suburb of Aranda. The third was by Neil Hermes who had chosen Black Mountain as the study site for his honours thesis. Much later, Neil produced *A Photographic Field Guide to the Birds of the Australian High Country* (2017), on which I was able to give some help. Bell and Hermes had both at different times studied 'mixed foraging flocks' on Black Mountain.

There is something about Black Mountain and Little Eagles. In 1954, two members of the CSIRO wildlife survey section, Francis Ratcliffe and John Calaby, contributed a zoology chapter to a small book, *The Australian Capital Territory as a Region*. They offered the

67

observation: 'A group of Raptores soaring over Black Mountain on a calm hot day a year or two ago included the wedge-tailed eagle, the little eagle, and the peregrine'. Recently, a nest of a Little Eagle pair, one of few remaining around the Canberra suburbs, was in use on the southern slopes.

Jerry Olsen told a remarkable eagle story. In 1966, a Little Eagle had been interfering with the rabbit research at Gungahlin. It was caught, banded, and removed to Jindabyne, about 150 km away. In the late 1980s, Jerry became aware of a banded female attending a nest on Black Mountain, but was unable to read the band. In October 1992, that Little Eagle was found dead near the nest, and found to be the bird banded at Gungahlin nearly 26 years earlier. At the time this was regarded as the oldest banded bird recovered in Australia. This is recounted in Jerry's *Australian High Country Raptors* (2014).

I found myself at the fringes of a quite fierce controversy about the status of the Little Eagle in the ACT. This revolved around the findings of Jerry Olsen and associates that there had in past years, in the 1980s and 1990s, been many more pairs of nesting Little Eagles than more recent observations suggested. My own contribution was summarised in a paper in *Canberra Bird Notes*, July 2018, pointing out that specific Little Eagle pairs were no longer found in their previous nesting territories in the northern part of the ACT. The controversy, fuelled by development plans for known nest sites, led to formation of a new research team to search for and monitor Little Eagle nesting activity in a more organized way. The search extended to private properties not previously investigated, and areas beyond the ACT boundaries. The conclusions from this work are yet to be finally published. It seems likely that the areas of suitable Little Eagle habitat in the ACT, being areas likely to feel the adverse impact of an expanding population, are too small to maintain an eagle population at previous levels. The future prospects for the species and its management need to be considered in a wider setting. That approach is in accordance with new arrangements for species conservation that attach importance to assessing conservation status at a national level.

Several locations in the ACT are popular for observing and photographing birds, but one spot is popular above all others. It is the section of Jerrabomberra Wetlands Nature Reserve accessible from the old Dairy Road, on the Fyshwick side. This takes in 'Kelly Swamp', named for the family that once had dairy cows there, to help provide Canberra with its milk supply. The walking trails take you through nearby plantings of various trees and shrubs. It was probably the sheer concentration of watchers that led to an out-of-range White-cheeked Honeyeater being picked up in those plantings. Even more unlikely was the appearance in due course of an apparent hybrid honeyeater, presumed to be a White-cheeked X New Holland Honeyeater. A hybrid, almost certainly the same bird, has been reported at the site each year from 2018 to 2021. A photographic project of mine followed its progress, and obtained evidence of successful breeding by it, with one or more New Holland Honeyeaters. This has been reported in *Canberra Bird Notes*.

Another interest, pursued over some years by video and still image, concerned the feeding methods of cockatoos. Easily captured on film were the Gang-gangs. These have a notch in the lower bill that holds the food item, say hawthorn fruit, or a eucalyptus seed-capsule, while it is split by the upper bill. The tongue manipulates the seed, for cracking between mandibles. In Canberra's suburbs you can get very close to feeding Gang-gangs. You can watch them from a couple of metres distance, as they rhythmically flick their large brown eyes from you to the next mouthful and back to you. Similar eye-flicking occurs with Glossy Black-Cockatoos, as they feed on the 'cones' of *Allocasuarina*. This notably non-glossy bird holds each seed-capsule like a small ice-cream cone as the great bill works its way down from the top.

In 2020, Glossies turned up in unusual places, such as eastern suburbs of Melbourne, and near Bourke, western NSW. This was attributed to the reliance of the species on inland remnant patches of *Allocasuarina*. When their specialized food habits could not be met, following a period of drought and fires, they spread out to find the essential food-trees wherever they could. Near Canberra, in Queanbeyan NSW, a family of three managed to live for a few weeks on plantings of an out-of-area species, *Allocasuarina distyla*.

The more common Yellow-tailed Blacks attack a range of food sources, at times concentrating on *Pinus radiata* cones. They tear apart the cone, extracting something that looks like a corn-flake (if you remember the breakfast cereal), and then, with that great bill, nip off the tiny seed, little larger than a tomato seed. When feeding on trees, those three species can be located by the sound of clicks and crunches and the patter of falling debris.

My interest in this subject was encouraged by Dominique Homberger of Louisiana State U, Baton Rouge, who has made regular visits to Australia, chiefly to look at cockatoos and parrots. Her ongoing part-time research concerns the evolution of bill size and shape as different populations make use of different food sources. At her suggestion, I made a couple of visits to Bourke, in winter, to get pictures of the Red-tailed Black-Cockatoos feeding on seeds of the White Cedar *Melia azderach*, an ornamental tree extensively planted in that town. It is a town that the strolling photographer will find very bad for barking dogs.

In August 2015, with Dominique and partner Ravi, I made a visit to Casterton, western Victoria, to see feeding on eucalyptus seeds by a different population of RTBCs. This was a subspecies that had been first formally described in 1988, unusually in a local journal, *Canberra Bird Notes*, by Schodde, Saunders and Homberger. The name chosen for the subspecies, *graptogyne*, was from the Greek for 'painted lady', being a reference to the colouring of the female. The endangered subspecies, amounting to about 1,500 individuals, is the subject of a recovery program. In the Casterton area, we were able to locate a feeding flock on each of two days, but only with the assistance of Richard Hill, who has been studying the population for more than 20 years.

Some members of COG engage in bird-banding, both as a hobby and with the aim of gathering useful information. Over the years, I was fortunate to be invited to several banding camp-outs on the eastern side of Weddin Mountains, near Grenfell, organised by Richard Allen. The effort Richard has applied to this ongoing project is quite extraordinary: 34 years, 181 trips (usually over a week-end), 16,000 individuals banded, 113 species. The location, a three-hour drive from Canberra, is a convenient place to look for 'western' species (babblers, apostlebird, turquoise parrot, spiny-cheeked honeyeater).

In the summer at end of 2019, we had a breeding influx of bird species in grasslands on the outskirts of Canberra, in particular Horsfield's Bushlark, and Brown Songlark, *Cincloramphus cruralis*. The latter is a wandering, endemic Australian species, although now designated as one of a broad grouping curiously labelled 'African warblers'. The distinctive male, much larger than the female, is usually photographed perched on a fence-post or a strand of barbed wire. However, the appearance of individuals varies markedly, according to sex, age, and season, and is not always well described or illustrated in books. I took the opportunity to photograph a range of plumages of numerous fence-perching individuals to illustrate variations to be found at the one time and place.

In October 2012, I was driving back from Geelong and made a detour towards Maldon, a historic township, still with signs of the presence of earlier Dabbs, who had operated small businesses there from the 1860s. For a couple of nights, I parked the campervan on John Pasquarelli's nature strip (Australian for road verge) at nearby Newstead. I had known Pasquarelli at law school in Melbourne. After that, in an unusual career, he was a patrol officer in NG (briefly), croc shooter, artefact dealer based on the Sepik, member of (PNG) parliament, tour guide, club and hotel manager, political staffer (his book: *The Pauline Hanson Story by the Man Who Knows* (1998)), successful artist, etc. I caught up with him at Newstead at the end of his painting period, when he was planning a move to Townsville. He is mentioned here because his painted subjects included magpies, and, as I found, he was yet another member of the magpie-feeding club.

I must include a bird-watching misfortune story. These happen to anyone who's been doing it long enough: a vehicle accident, loss of equipment, maybe even personal injury. I've had all three. When I drove to Sydney to give a talk at the museum, I parked at the art gallery to stretch my legs for a few minutes and came back to find the Prado broken into and the laptop gone, with several months of unsaved images. Perhaps more interesting was BEING BITTEN BY A FOX WHILE BIRDWATCHING. I was in Callum Brae nature reserve when I saw a fox that seemed to be in difficulty. It was dragging a metal rabbit trap attached to a foot, and as I watched it became entangled in a fence. It was a beautiful young animal, so without thinking I put a hand on the trap to release it. The bite left me with puncture wounds over my right hand. One was through a nail that had to be removed, so an inconvenient result from a moment's carelessness. In Australia, you are much more likely to be bitten by an injured flying fox than an actual fox, although neither is a likely event while birdwatching, provided you keep your mind on what you are doing. We have both kinds of animal in Canberra.

Now to that other great dimension of birdia, the world of books.

Artists' Corner: Above, a birdy Christmas card from 2010, and a birdwatcher sculpture (sculptor unknown); right, carved bird figures from New Guinea; below, a memento from New Guinea days, the 'F' painting (frog, falcon, Frenchman etc); John Pasquarelli in his Newstead house with magpie painting.

XII

Books

Alice was beginning to get very tired of sitting by her sister on the bank, and of having nothing to do: once or twice she had peeped into the book her sister was reading, but it had no pictures or conversations in it, "and what is the use of a book", thought Alice, "without pictures or conversations?"

—Alice's Adventures in Wonderland, first lines.

There are books about birds, and books about bird books. In one of the latter, I find the following:

Since the war, the increase in mobility and leisure together with the impact of natural history television programmes have impelled many people, who are not bird watchers in the accepted sense, to buy a bird book of some description. This interest has resulted in a flood of ornithological publications …

That appears in *Birds, Men and Books: A literary history of ornithology*, by Peter Tate, a book published in 1986, 41 years after 'the war'. At that time, the flood had hardly begun, relatively speaking.

Accumulating bird books is a hobby in itself. I am not a collector in the sense of owning books worth thousands of dollars, but I do have too many bird books. They extend across four rooms. Some are well-thumbed, some seldom opened. Those I mention in these pages cover only a small fraction of the books within those rooms.

Sometimes I can't find a book I am sure I have somewhere, so I need to go to a library for a copy, or even buy another one. They have come from many sources: used bookshops of the world, museum shops, Andrew Isles, online purchases, copies for review. Sometimes people give them to me. My next-door neighbours went on a cruise to South Africa and brought back a little book for me, in return for watering their garden. It is *Birds of Mauritius, Rodrigues & Islets* (2018) by Naraimsamy Ramen, obviously picked up in the course of the voyage, as students of geography will appreciate.

At the start of a wander by the bookshelves, we might note two useful publications about Australian birds. The first is known as 'HANZAB', in full: *Handbook of Australian, New Zealand & Antarctic Birds*, organised by RAOU, published by Oxford University Press, Australia. This appeared in seven volumes between 1990 and 2006. It is an Australasian counterpart of the nine-volume *Birds of the Western Palearctic* (1977–1994). It is a great dump of unevaluated compressed information, pointing you to sources to be followed up when you have a serious interest in any species in the area covered. A shortcoming is that the early volumes are now quite old, and even the later ones can be out of date given the pace of research these days. The second publication, less well known, is for those with an interest in bird conservation. It is *The Action Plan for Australian Birds*, a substantial volume updated about every 10 years. There have been four editions since 1992, the fourth being a very large book indeed. Stephen Garnett has been the co-ordinator, under sponsorship of the Australian government and Birdlife Australia.

To try to introduce some order into a vast subject, bird books, broadly, have three kinds of contents: pictures, facts and stories. Some offer (a) mainly illustrations or photographs (pictures); others (b) mainly information or technical discussion (facts); others again (c) mainly history, anecdotes or biography (stories). As an example of (a) pictures, or at least 'mainly pictures', I would name John Lewin's *Birds of New South Wales* (1838), of which I have a facsimile. This has 26 colour plates and very few facts. On similar lines, I have a one-volume republishing of John Gould's *Hummingbirds* (1849–1861), which has 418 full-page plates and only 74 pages of notes. These days, you are likely to open it only for the pictures.

John Gould achieved fame for his *Birds of Australia* (1840–1848) and other lavish pictorial productions. In 1865, he produced a *Handbook* about Australian birds in two volumes, 1,265 pages. There are no pictures in this, just a lot of information. For his time, Gould knew a great deal about Australian birds. He often speculated about what was yet be learnt. With respect to the Northern Shoveler, he had to ask his 'ornithological readers both in Australia and Europe to take [his] word for the occasional appearance of the bird in Australia'. His brother-in-law, Stephen Coxen, had shown him a skin, but that was eaten by a rat before Gould could put it in a safe place. He was unable to find another specimen. This was his advice to Australian birdwatchers: 'To this subject, therefore, I recommend the attention of those in Australia, who will doubtless meet with the bird some day when the country is subject to partial inundation'.

According to HANZAB, the first 'authenticated and acceptable record' of the species in Australia was from Louth, NSW, 136 years later, in 1975. It is now regarded in Australia as a rare but regular vagrant, with a full entry in the *Australian Bird Guide* (2017, 2019).

Most popular bird books fall within the intermediate description 'picture-based and informative'. With respect to these, there has been a progression over time. After the expensive offerings of Gould and Audubon, different ways were found to illustrate bird books for a broader distribution. In the United Kingdom, Archibald Thorburn was commissioned to create most of the paintings for Lord Lilford's *Coloured Figures of the Birds of the British Isles* (1885–1897). The same paintings were used for *The Birds of the British Isles and Their Eggs* (T. A Coward, 1920). Although in two smallish volumes, with a third added in 1926, this was declared to be 'a Handy Pocket Guide, in which each bird is represented by a coloured illustration to aid identification'. The same paintings, reduced in size even further, appeared in 1936 in a condensed version of the three volumes edited by Enid Blyton under the title, *Birds of the Wayside and Woodland*.

In 1896 came a four-volume *Handbook to the Birds of Great Britain*, authored by R. Bowdler Sharpe of the British Museum and intended for popular use, but with a museum flavour. In the preface, he reviewed the 'excellent books' that had already been produced on the subject, referring to the pending Lord Lilford work, and to 'the popularity of Yarrell's "History of British Birds" with its exquisite little woodcuts'. The illustrations in Sharpe's book appear to be recolourings, by chromolithography, of the engravings used in the Naturalist's Library some 40 years earlier.

The five-volume *Handbook of British Birds* (1938–1941) by H F Witherby and others carried plates mostly attributed to a Dutch landscape painter Marinus Adrianus Koekkoek the Younger, originally painted for a book on birds of The Netherlands. There were also paintings by H. Gronvold, G. E. Lodge and Peter Scott. The plates were reproduced in reduced form in a one-volume *Popular Handbook of British Birds* by Peter Hollom. The first edition came out just before the 1954 Peterson field guide that he co-authored.

For North America, here are three books that show increasing sophistication in meeting popular demand. First, *Birds of America* (1917), the work of various authors: 'over 1000 pages … over 1000 pictures including 514 bird portraits in natural colour by Louis

Agassis Fuertes'. This contains many black-and-white photos of birds, and some of bird photographers in challenging situations. The National Geographic Society's *Book of Birds* was published 1932–1937, 'with 950 color portraits by Major Allan Brooks'. The many black-and-white photos show that equipment was improving. There is a chapter on the Cornell University expedition of 1935 to film and record rare birds. One achievement was the first photograph ever taken of a nesting pair of Ivory-billed Woodpeckers. Another photo shows mules hauling a farm wagon with the recording equipment through a flooded forest to the Ivorybill nest, four mules being required for the purpose. The third book had appeared in 1925 as *Natural History of the Birds of Eastern and Central America*. The 1939 edition explained that changes under headings 'Identification' and 'Voice' were 'adaptations from Roger Tory Peterson's "Field Guide to the Birds", which every bird student should include in his equipment'. Four additional plates by Peterson were included. The age of the modern identification guide had arrived.

In Australia, the story of the picture-based bird book after Gould must note the contribution of Gracius Joseph Broinowski. The unhappy tale of his *Birds of Australia* involved Henry Parkes and Edmund Barton. It is recounted by Keith Hindwood in *Australian Zoologist* 13 (4) 357. Published in 1889, the book of 303 chromolithographs, in 40 parts, could be purchased for £24/0/0, bound in cloth. After that came the well-known smaller, popular books with famously long runs of revisions and reprintings: Leach (originally 2011), Cayley (1932).

For Australia, just before the 'modern field guides' came the large *Australian Birds* by Robin Hill (1967). In this groundbreaking publication, the pictures were striking and attractive, Robin himself being a trained book-designer. 'I hope this splendid book will have the success it deserves', said the Duke of Edinburgh in the foreword. It certainly did. In 1971, Hill relocated to the US, pursuing a career as a portraitist and birdwatching yachtsman. I recently made contact with him by email, out of curiosity about what he might be doing. He was particularly pleased with another large book, *The Waterfowl of North America* (1987). When I mentioned I had difficulty finding it in Australia, he generously sent me a copy of it. It is indeed a handsome book, perhaps 'magnificent', the word used by the Duke of Edinburgh in yet another foreword.

In a lengthy 'Artist's Preface' Robin Hill discusses whether bird illustration is Art.

'An artist makes art of any subject. … I will step out onto thin ice: I think that from Audubon to the present, there have not been a dozen true artists painting wildlife as their chief subjects. What these few have done is to quicken the world of nature with a spirit that rises from a wellspring within each of them. Their creatures, like Cezanne's apples, have a glow of inner life which sets them apart from mere illustrations.'

Books about Australian birds by artist Robin Hill.

A satisfying blend of pictures-with-facts can be found in the books produced by Joe Forshaw. I have lost count of these. First came *Australian Parrots* in 1969, that edition relying mainly on photos. The next was a very large book, *Parrots of the World* (1973), with the paintings of the much-admired William Cooper. My wife gave me a copy of that, so it was on the shelf in Port Moresby. I first met Joe about 10 years later in Canberra, in connection with some environmental law issue. I told him I thought *Parrots of the World* was a fine book, although rather heavy. He said I was lucky to have a copy. In the book, Joe says the idea for it came, when he was in the American Museum of Natural History in 1964, from Tom Gilliard. Some people seem to pop up everywhere.

In *The Birds of Paradise and Bower Birds* (1977), William Cooper was named first on the title page for his striking art, with the text credited to Forshaw and Cooper. You can only agree with the dust-jacket: 'In the best tradition of fine bird books it gives pleasure to the eye and satisfaction to the mind'. There were several more Forshaw productions, including *Pigeons and Doves in Australia* (2017 – Forshaw and Cooper), and, with other artists, *Vanished and Vanishing Parrots* (2017 – with Frank Knight) and *Trogons* (2009 – with Albert Earl Gilbert).

A book of a similar style, combining authoritative text with art, is *The Fairy-Wrens* (1984) by Dick Schodde, illustrations by Richard Weatherly. This is not a book I own, but these comments will be incomplete if I don't mention it. Several of the illustrations, and some of the story of its creation, appear in Weatherly's recent *Brush With Birds* (2020).

As an example of books that are confined to '(b) facts', I am inclined to point to Ernst Mayr's 1941 *List of New Guinea Birds*, to which I have referred already. This has no story and no pictures. It does have a map, but I would regard that as information. A similar feature, a map, is also included with that important non-pictorial 1926 publication, *The Official Checklist of the Birds of Australia*. Other taxonomic lists will be credible candidates, but I choose to nominate, as the best example on my shelves of a 'facts' book, *Distribution and Taxonomy of the Birds of the World* (1990) by Charles Sibley and Burt Monroe, Jr. This, really a checklist, has 1,111 pages, no story as I would define the word, and no picture, just a few maps at the back. A bird does appear on the dust jacket. I am reluctant to remove the protective plastic to see if there is any picture on the binding, because that would risk loss of the errata slip, which contains several additional facts, for example with respect to *Cisticola juncidis* 'New Guinea' can be removed from the places where that species does not occur.

I will spend a little more time on the 'story' books. To indicate the range of these, I start with a few Australian offerings. Hubert Whittell published his *Literature of Australian Birds* in 1954. Even then, he could write of 'the vast literature' on the subject of Australian birds which 'can be appreciated by perusal of the pages which follow'. There followed 780 pages of small print. A supplement, by Tess Kloot, was published in 1995. Whittell's book certainly offers facts about its subject (literature), but it also contains a lot of stories in the form of biography, not only in the early historical narrative but in entries on selected authors.

Libby Robin's *The Flight of the Emu* (2001) was written to coincide with the centenary of the Royal Australasian Ornithologists' Union (RAOU). Here we come up against that 'birding' point again. According to the blurb on the dust-jacket, the book 'tells the story of Australian birding in the twentieth century'. In fact, the book is mainly about the scientific side, so far as RAOU has contributed to it. However, the blurb will not let go of the lighter theme. It concludes with:

> 'Birdos' have a great sense of humour; and the pleasure and fun of bird watching, whether it be serious scientific observation, 'twitching' or just a relaxing hobby, comes through strongly in this clear, friendly and richly-illustrated book.

In recent years Penny Olsen has had a remarkable output of books about birds, extending to some 30 volumes to the present time, in a range of formats and styles. Having mentioned Neville W. Cayley, I should draw attention to Penny's biographies of Neville W., and his father, in *Cayley & Son* (2013). This is a book of stories and pictures. Of some interest to me is the foreword by that seductive book vendor, Andrew Isles *[my comments added]*:

> As a mustard-keen ten-year-old interested in all things birds, I discovered *What Bird Is That?* by Neville William Cayley in the school library. *[Me too, but different school]* Soon after, it became the first bird book I ever purchased. Every night I would immerse myself in exotic birds from remote places … *[well, exotic places in Australia, anyway.]*

Another of Penny's many books should be mentioned, *Feather and Brush* (2001). This is about artists, many well-known, some less so, who have taken Australian birds as their subject, making yet another satisfying blend of pictures and stories. A revised and greatly expanded edition has appeared recently.

My next book is an unusual but substantial contribution to the literature. Ian Mason and Gilbert Pfitzner have produced *Passions in Ornithology: A Century of Australian Egg Collectors* (2020). I was given a copy for purpose of review. The book has entries for some 300 of 'the most prominent oological Australian collectors' – nearly 500 pages of them. There is a much longer list of 'incidental collectors'. Some of the collectors are well-known in Australian ornithology. However, the great majority of entries relate to people whose claim to inclusion is simply that they had a significant record of collecting bird eggs. As shown in the appendices, their enthusiasm sometimes extended to detailed record-keeping. As the authors note: 'In a number of cases, data collected by these oologists … is more detailed than that recorded by amateur birdwatchers and even professional ornithologists'.

With the book comes a CD containing appendices, with correspondence, record cards, other original material, and book references.

A contrasting kind of story is to be found in two small volumes by Brigadier Hugh Officer about his bird observing experiences. In one, *Recollections of a Birdwatcher* (1978), he speaks of the birds around Simla, the hill station in India. 'I made the fortunate discovery that my tailor there, A.E. Jones, was one of the great authorities on sub-Himalayan birds… I still have his pamphlet, *The Common Birds of Simla*.' Andrew Isles must have acquired Hugh Officer's library, by which route that pamphlet by A. E. Jones now sits on my own desk. I had been puzzled by the inscription on the cover 'H. R. Officer, Carignano, 22 May to 1 June 1942.' 'Carignano' must be Italian. Why was an Italian location, in wartime, inscribed on a book about Simla birds? Happily, the travel information on the internet helps you solve all sorts of mysteries, as follows in this case:

> At 3km from Mashobra is Carignano, a picnic spot that was a villa of Chevalier Federico Peliti, an Italian photographer in India from the times of Queen Victoria, who named it in honour of his native town Carignano near Turin in Italy. The villa was transformed to a weekend resort in 1920 …

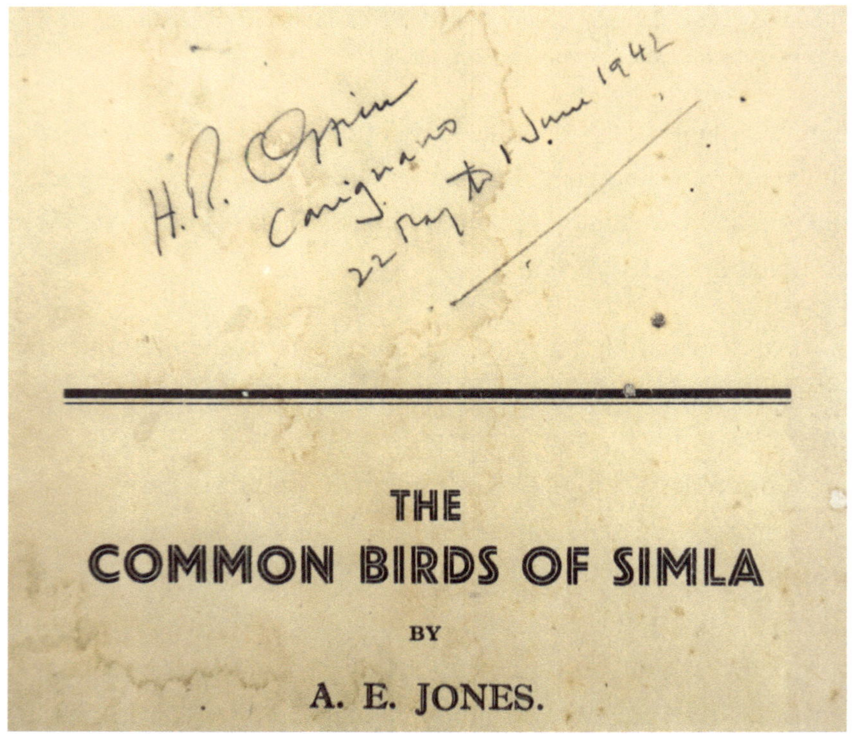

1942 inscription on *The Common Birds of Simla.*

I owe to Andrew Isles an even more perplexing puzzle. In his shop, I bought a small pre-used volume *Japanese Birds*, published in 1941, and number 35 in a 'Tourist Library' evidently intended to help welcome English-speaking visitors to Japan. This bears the inscription inside the front cover:

Alec: Our fellow ornithologist F.M. Lord Alanbrooke was most anxious to let you have this souvenir of our local researches – with phosphatic greetings for Xmas 1945. Massey Stanley

Lord Alanbrooke, the wartime military leader, was a well-known birdwatcher. At war's end, in November 1945, Alanbrooke visited Japan to confer with General MacArthur. A few days later his RAF aircraft flew on to Australia, landing at Darwin on 24 November and then to Melbourne. Alanbrooke's diary for the 26th records: 'visited a Bird Sanctuary and dined at Government House sitting up until midnight talking to the Duke of Gloucester'. We know from a press report that the 'sanctuary' was the one at Healesville.

Massey Stanley was a journalist. From 1941 to 1946, he was based in Melbourne editing an army educational journal. He also made some overseas visits as a war correspondent. He was one of the first journalists to visit post-war Japan, reporting from Hiroshima in October 1945. No written evidence can be found that he had a special interest in birds, but there is certainly evidence that he had a keen interest in the Australian bush among many other things.

Who then was 'Alec', the recipient of the Japanese bird book? In 1945, Alec Chisholm (1890–1977) was probably Australia's leading public ornithologist. (I use 'public' in the sense used in the current phrase 'public intellectual'.) He was another journalist, who, as Libby Robin records, 'edited major dailies in the 1930s and early 1940s, became editor of *Who's Who* from the mid-1940s, and assembled the mammoth *Australian Encyclopedia* in the 1950s'. Along with Crosbie Morrison he was one of the 'high-profile journalists' who 'made ornithology's concerns mainstream'. In the entry for Alec Chisholm in the *Australian Dictionary of Biography*, Tess Kloot says: 'When dignitaries went birdwatching, he was called upon to act as guide: he would count among his acquaintances … Lord Alanbrooke …'

When, before Christmas 1945, could Alanbrooke, Massey Stanley, and Chisholm have been birdwatching together? Most likely over those couple of days in Melbourne in November, perhaps on that visit to Healesville. For a time in 1945, Chisholm was press liaison officer for the Duke of Gloucester. Alanbrooke must have brought one or more copies of *Japanese Birds* from Japan for gifts. 'Phosphatic greetings' remains a mystery.

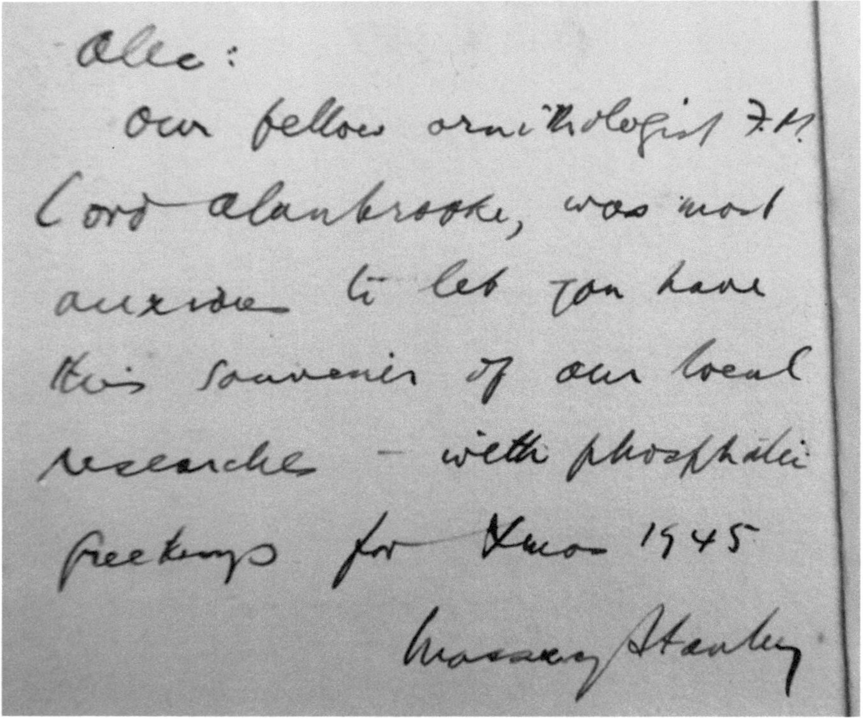

1945 inscription in *Japanese Birds*.

XIII

Quests and challenges

'Search for (X)' books are a particular kind of story writing. *Search for the Spiny Babbler*, by American ornithologist Dillon Ripley, is about a visit to Nepal in 1948. An earlier book by the same author, *Trail of the Money Bird*, was really a travel book with the main focus being collection of bird specimens in north-western (The Netherlands) New Guinea in 1936/1937. Ripley would have been 23 at the time. 'Money bird' was the name used by Malays (presumably in Malay) for the King Bird of Paradise which seems to carry shiny discs at the ends of wire-like plumes. In the *Spiny Babbler* book, the author manages to shoot one of a flock of brown thrush-like birds which turns out to be the (then) little-known Spiny Babbler, *Acanthoptila nipalensis.*

There are no pictures in that book. Instead, they are to be found in a National Geographic article by Ripley, *Peerless Nepal – A Naturalist's Paradise*, issue of January 1950. The photos include a famous one of a Mercedes car being carried over a river crossing. 'Some 60 coolies, moving to the rhythm of a chant, balance it on long poles.' No Spiny Babblers other than that deceased one, with its flock, were found on the expedition. It is brought to life in the article in a striking painting by Walter A. Weber over the text: 'Spiny Babbler, lost to science for 106 years is pictured among flowering Rhododendrons'.

There is even less success in *The Search for the Pink-headed Duck* (1991) by Rory Nugent. In the search, the author, we are told, 'bought a thirteen-foot skiff and became the first person to paddle the Brahmaputra from Burma to Bangladesh'. There are many disappointing moments: 'The next morning I inspect every flock we pass, looking for the pink duck. Twice I spot a misfit among the widgeons, but the duck doesn't sparkle pink when it turns in the sunlight.' Another 'odyssey' duck book, with a different kind of quarry, is *The Curse of the Labrador Duck* (2009), by Glen Chilton. If I say it's mainly about museums, and says of the duck 'never as famous as the Passenger Pigeon, the Dodo, or the Great Auk', you will guess where that one takes its readers.

Fortunately for painters of extinct bird species there are usually enough surviving fragments for a version to be produced that is good enough for people who have never seen the bird. In exceptional cases, the artist might have might have had the good fortune to see the bird in life. Here are convincing versions of the Labrador Duck by Audubon and by Robin Hill.

The 'looking for' theme is taken up by prolific author Peter Mathiessen in *The Birds of Heaven: Travels with Cranes* (2003). The author gives us separate stories about his experiences searching for each of the 15 remaining species of crane, over a period of more than 10 years.

A different kind of search is *On the Road with John James Audubon* (1984, Mary Durant and Michael Harwood). It is a search for the places mentioned by Audubon in his own writings. The narrative is full of descriptions of scenes, birds, and people. It follows Audubon's travels from his first home in Pennsylvania as a 19-year-old just arrived in America (1804) to his last home in then-rural Manhattan, overlooking the Hudson River. I have mentioned my experience of a Barred Owl. Audubon said of this species:

> At the approach of night, their cries are heard proceeding from every part of the forests around the plantations … and they respond to each other in tones so strange that one might imagine some extraordinary fete about to take place among them.

Durant and Harwood also discuss the call of this owl:

> "Who cooks for you? Who cooks for *you*-all?" The questions ring clear, the interpretation you'll find in just about anything you may read about the barred owl, whether in a signs-of-spring editorial in

The New York Times or in a scientific essay. In Audubon's day this reading of the barred owl's cry had evidently not become commonplace. He described it merely as *whah, whah, whah, whah-aa.*

Audubon's presentation of a Barred Owl, with something going on, as in many of Audubon's compositions.

Then there is the theme of competitive personal-bird-listing. *Wild America* (1955) is by James Fisher ('England's leading populariser of natural history') and Roger Tory Peterson ('his American opposite-number'). It is about 100 days in 1953 when those two friends travelled for 30,000 miles to see, film and write about the natural history of North America. Along the way, they try to break the then modest single-year record for North American bird species. They do this easily, even in the limited period, Fisher briefly holding the record when he records an Upland Plover at Martha's vineyard. After that, for the next wave of record-seekers, things became much more competitive, as shown by the continuing story of the North American Big Year[3].

Of course, there are 'Big Year' books.

The Big Year (2004) by Mark Obmaskic is about the year 1998 when three birders set out to break the North America record in competition with one another. It is written by a journalist, in the rollicking style of a journalist out to sell a story to the general public. (I say 'rollicking' because the word is used three times in the promotional blurbs in my copy.) It was translated into a 2011 film under the same name. This was not a box-office success.

Another book from North America is *Kingbird Highway* (1997) by Kenn Kaufman. I am mentioning this a little out of order because an 'afterword' in a later edition (2006) looks back on the Obmaskic book, making the reasonable comment that its 'vivid play-by-play' of the action' is 'perhaps a little too vivid'. (That was still too early for a comment on the

---

[3] See https://en.wikipedia.org/wiki/Big_year; https://en.wikipedia.org/wiki/American_Birding_Association, https://en.wikipedia.org/

2011 movie, unfortunately.) *Kingbird Highway* is a significant addition to the literature. It was first published 24 years after Kaufman's year of hitch-hiking around North America to record 666 bird species, a feat performed by the 19-year-old with practically no money. The book is about birds, and also people, mainly enthusiastic young birders of the 1970s ('… we were not birdwatching. We were birding, and that made all the difference'.) The book ends on a reflective, questioning note, continued in the afterword: 'My big year started with a quest for a birding record but ended in a quest for something else.' On the back of my edition is a small photo of Kenn Kaufman (19 years) with Roger Tory Peterson (64 years), taken at the first convention of the American Bird Association. Kenn was a non-paying attender, in a good sense.

Perhaps the Library of Congress has the last word on the birding/bird-watching issue. On the page of *Kingbird Highway* with the publishing information appears the book's formal subject, taken from a standard list. This, in short, is 'Bird watching'. According to the Library of Congress list of subjects (42nd edition, April 2020), 'Bird watching' is to be used rather than, but to include, 'Birding'.

The Big Twitch (2005) by Sean Dooley is an entertaining book about an Australian Big Year. It also has quite a lot of information about birds, and about Australia. The year was 2004, same year the Obmaskic book was published. Like Kenn Kaufman, Dooley is clearly an amiable person, with no shortage of friends. These are a big help to him in getting to his remarkable total of 703 species. In *An Australian Birding Year* (2020) R. Bruce Richardson covers a 12-month period in 2015/2016. This is a chatty account, with photos, of bird-seeking travels around the country by an American couple. As in the Dooley book a list of recorded species is given (here 640), with dates and locations.

World-bird-ticking is a subject that lends itself to a book. There are so many birds and people out there that several books can be written without the same ones (birds or people) being mentioned more than once. In 2008, Alan Davies and Ruth Miller set out to break the record of 3,662 set in 1989 by *Checklist*-author Jim Clements. The book, *The Biggest Twitch* (with a nod here to Sean Dooley), mentions a lot of both birds and people. The record was broken with a 'Bluebonnet Parrot' on the golf course at Griffith NSW on 31 October.

Birding Without Borders is an informative and light-hearted account by Noah Strycker of his year 2015. The aim of this 30-year-old American was to tick 5,000 species, visiting places around the world. Imagine the photograph accompanied by this text: 'Birding the world requires a stack of field guides far too heavy to pack. I scanned all of these into digital files for reference during the year'. The photo shows Noah standing beside a column of stacked books, by my count 58 in number but lacking, so far as I can see, anything that would be useful in Australia. He must have bought his Australian field guide when here. This was where he ticked, in 15 days, 432 of his total of 6,042 species, all listed according to country and date.

I mentioned Noah's feat to Frank O'Connor, who on a Christmas morning had 'birded the mulga' with him, in Western Australia. Frank had expected to find 80 new species for the super-lister but most were ticked by the time Perth was reached. Finding Australian birds for overseas visitors is easy enough, but finding 'new birds' can be difficult.

XIV

Some bird book people of times past

A favourite book is *Portrait of a Wilderness* (1958) by Guy Mountfort, co-author of that 1954 field guide. It is about expeditions to the Coto Donana, a bird-rich corner of Andalusia. Among many photos are two, black and white, on one page. The upper one shows Roger Peterson, with Eric Hosking and others, 'taking long-range pictures at the heronry'. Eric Hosking, the most famous bird photographer of his day, gives his own account of that expedition in his autobiography *An Eye for a Bird* (1970). He also explains his book's title, referring to loss of an eye to a Tawny Owl which he was photographing in 1937.

In *Portrait*, the lower photo is of a bowler-hatted Lord Alanbrooke, who 'obtained many unique cinema films of rare birds during the expeditions of 1956 and 1957'. This is another case where the National Geographic is hot on the heels of the book-author. There is an article about the expedition by Roger Tory Peterson in the issue of March 1958: 'Rare Birds Flock to Spain's Marismas'.

As becomes evident, there is a certain amount of inter-weaving in the stories related in the literature. I have a book that I bought in London in 1965 at Foyles bookshop. It is *Pirates and Predators* (1959) by Colonel Richard Meinertzhagen. This is an unusual kind of book, with many first-hand anecdotes about predatory bird behaviour. 'I have seen the goshawk kill on five occasions and have not yet seen an unsuccessful hunt.' Each of the kills is then recounted. Over subsequent years, I wondered from time to time who Colonel Meinertzhagen was. A comprehensive answer came with Mark Cocker's *Richard Meinertzhagen: Soldier, Scientist & Spy* (1989). Among many other things, this deals with misdemeanours involving collections and papers in the British Museum, apparently settled in 1954 when RM handed over his vast collection of specimens, and was made an Honorary Associate.

Long after Meinertzhagen had regained favour at the British Museum, and after his death in 1967, it was found on examining his collections that he had been guilty of a range of fraudulent conduct over a long period. The story of his many thefts of skins, and forgeries, received publicity in the 1990s. Some of this is told in *The Meinertzhagen Mystery: The life and legend of a colossal fraud* (2007), by Brian Garfield. Meanwhile, of interest to Australians, Meinertzhagen had been portrayed as a war hero in the 1987 film *The Light Horsemen*. Meinertzhagen, played by Anthony Andrews, makes a success of the charge at Beersheba by diverting the Turkish defenders through an elaborate feat of disinformation.

When at the Washington embassy, I regularly visited Ottawa in the course of work. At one bookshop, the owner recommended a little volume, *The Birds of Brewery Creek* (1947) by Malcolm MacDonald. The author was son of former British Prime Minister Ramsay MacDonald, and himself a former MP. The book was about a year of casual bird observing, in Ottawa, on and around the named creek, 'truly a paradise for an ornithologist'. Unexpectedly, according to the dust-jacket: 'Bird watching as a hobby is in the great tradition of British statesmanship.' At the time of the observing, the author was the wartime UK High Commissioner to Canada. MacDonald later became High Commissioner in New Delhi about which experience he wrote *Birds in my Indian Garden* (1961). He also wrote the text for *Birds in the Sun* (1962), also about India. The photographer for both books was Christina Loke. Macdonald quotes Salim Ali, 'the greatest of Indian ornithologists', as saying of her photos, 'Many of them are the finest pictures of Indian birds in existence'. Roger Tory Peterson, from the mildly sexist viewpoint of the day, ranked her 'ahead of any other female bird photographer in the world'.

Salim Ali has a small place in Australian ornithology. In his autobiography, *The Fall of a Sparrow* (1985), he draws attention to letters he received, addressed to *Mrs* Salim Ali (who had died in 1939), expressing sympathy for his death. This had been announced at the 1974 International Ornithological Congress in Canberra. One letter was from Guy Mountfort on behalf of the British Ornithologists' Union. Another was from a Japanese delegate who reported that the Executive Committee had observed one-minute silent prayer for the repose of his soul.

In his autobiography, Salim Ali draws some threads together. In 1937, Salim Ali made an expedition to Afghanistan with Meinertzhagen, 'one of the most colourful, original and, in many ways, likeable characters that ornithology introduced me to'. They noted particularly the migration that was in progress such as 'the unbelievable hordes of Rosy Pastor from the Indian plains to their nesting grounds in Turkestan'. However, Salim Ali's best birding mate was Loke Wan Tho, to whom he devotes a chapter. 'The near identity of our outlook and interests brought us closer together than any of my latter-day friends.' The first wife of Wan Tho, himself a noted photographer, was Christina Loke. Salim had a higher opinion of Christina's photography than her 'temperament and outlook'.

After his early expeditions in India with Salim Ali, Wan Tho, in 1952, 'undertook the most difficult expedition' he had ever attempted. This was to the moss-forests of New Guinea, and is described in *A Company of Birds* (1957, foreword by Malcolm MacDonald). He was prompted to take the trip by a meeting in Singapore with Fred Shaw Mayer, who was on his way to London with a collection of bird skins. His camp was near Nondugl. One of Wan Tho's photos is of a female 'bird of paradise' at the nest. Contrary to the initial identification, this was later identified by Ernst Mayr as *Cnemophilus macgregorii*, later, although not permanently, known as the Crested Bird of Paradise. In the book, the view is expressed that this was the first photograph of a bird of paradise at the nest. It is a sign of the fashion of the time that all of Wan Tho's 18 New Guinea bird photos, except one of dependant young, are of birds at the nest. One photo is of Belford's Melidectes *Melidectes belfordi*, where Wan Tho seems to have got in first with the English name 'Spectacled Honeyeater'.

In a recent article in the online *Mumbai Mirror*, Indian ornithologist Bikram Grewal has written about the friendships of Salim Ali that helped contribute to his expertise. Three names are put forward: Loke Wan Tho, S. Dillon Ripley, and Richard Meinertzhagen. As I have never been to India for serious bird-observing, my interest in Salim Ali requires a word of explanation. The answer is in his books. I have five different editions of *The Book of Indian Birds* and several of his books on regions of India and most volumes of the *Handbook* that he wrote with Dillon Ripley. To me, these are part of an intriguing historical progression. Together with early books produced by the British in India and the later glossy volumes for the travelling ticker, they tell a story of growing appreciation of the bird life of the sub-continent – and of improving skills in making pictures of it. My father spent some years in India during and just after World War 2, so that might have had something to do with it also.

XV

Field Guides and some questions of geography

Birding is the most literate of outdoor pastimes: few birders would ever consider going into the woods without a trusty field guide.

—Mark Obmascik, *The Big Year* (2004)

To me, that is not an accurate statement. More accurately, few birders *who need a field guide* would go into the woods without one. However, there is no doubt that the popularity of bird-observing has grown largely because of the availability of comprehensive modern guides (a) for the beginner, to local birds and (b) for the travelling bird-observer, to birds further afield. I have a lot of field guides. There are several reasons for this. One is that I used to buy successive editions, keeping them all. Another is that I do not buy field guides only to places I intend to visit. I buy field guides about places I will never visit, and read them like paperback novels. With the foreign language ones I look at the pictures, and guess what the text might say.

I once had the aim of owning a field guide illustration of every bird species, but that has been overtaken by other developments. It was possible to fill gaps between regional guides with books such as *Seabirds: an identification guide* (1983), by Peter Harrison, and *Shorebirds:*

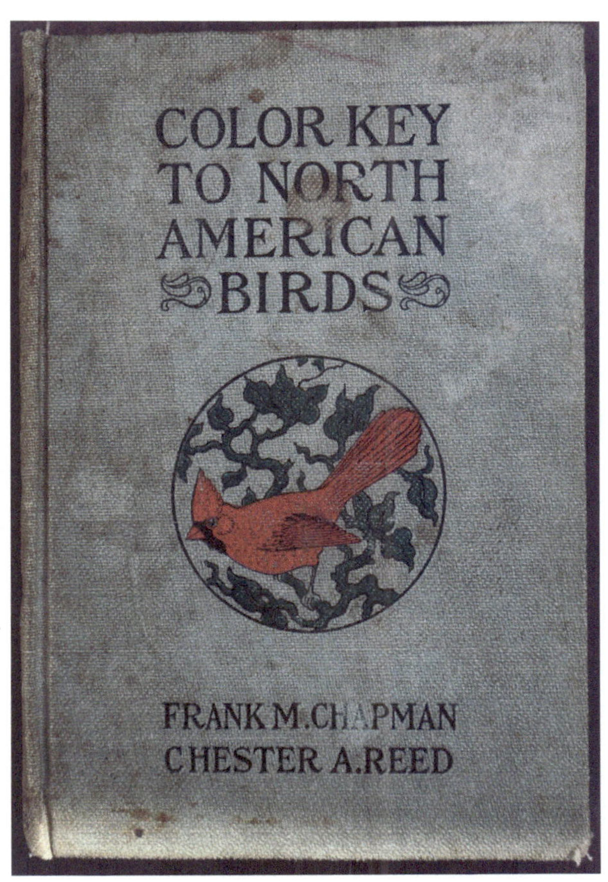

No longer carried into the woods. A well-thumbed copy of the *Color Key* of 1903, by Frank Chapman and Chester Reed. A great advance as a help with bird identification.

an identification guide (1986), by P. Hayman, J. Marchant, and T. Prater. There was a Helm series and a Houghton Mifflin series. Later came the Oxford University Press *Bird Families of the World* series, but those contained too much information for my purpose, and were an expensive way to pursue my objective.

The importance of the first 1934 Peterson guide, to eastern North American birds, as the first 'modern field guide', is widely acknowledged. Stephen Moss, in *A Bird in the Bush: a social history of birdwatching* (2004), makes the point clearly enough. There had been earlier field guides, in several countries, but not so well-presented or informative, with an emphasis on separating similar species. That is the main respect in which Cayley's *What Bird Is That?* (published earlier, in 1931) fell short. If Cayley had arranged all his birds by relationship rather than habitat, he would probably have done a better job of drawing attention to small differences between similar species. Compare the work of Lilian Medland for what might have been a rival guide to Australian birds. (Published as *Seen but Not Heard* (2014), text by Christobel Mattingley.) Some of her plates are better aids to identification than Cayley's, and better than her contributions to *Birds of New Guinea*.

Stephen Moss explains the background to that 1954 European guide. It began as a chance encounter at, of all places, Hawk Mountain, Pennsylvania, when Peterson met Guy Mountfort. Over five years, the authors, including Philip Hollom, travelled around Europe to get field experience of more than 500 species. As Moss says, '*A Field Guide to the Birds of Britain and Europe* was light years ahead of its rival', *The Pocket Guide to British Birds* (1952), by Richard Fitter and Richard Richardson.

Mark Cocker tells the story more fully, starting with his view of Richard Richardson as 'one of the most popular, the most revered, the most remembered birders from the second half of the twentieth century, possibly from the whole century'. In the *Pocket Guide* he 'offered criteria for identifying birds which had never been considered as readily separable before'. He was 'above all a sophisticated field observer'.

> Trouble was, so too were Guy Mountfort and Philip Hollom and their American friend, the artist Roger Tory Peterson … Just two years after Richard's plates appeared, the three of them produced the closest thing to a revolution in bird books, a work called *A Field Guide to the Birds of Britain and Europe*. Richardson's plates were good, but Peterson's were better.

The bold, accurate colours and diagrammatic formula of the American artist's birds completely eclipsed the Englishman's achievement. They captured exactly what the beginner birder needs to achieve an identification.

It was not until 1970 that there was something along the same lines for Australia, with the first Peter Slater guide.

I have a chunky soft-cover book titled *A Guide to the Birds of Columbia* (1986), by Steven Hilty and William Brown. It covers all 1,695 species that had been recorded in Columbia to that point in time. As a precaution, it describes separately a further 133 species that 'probably occur in Columbia' but had not yet been recorded there. 'A few of these can be found on the south bank of the Amazon opposite Columbia but are not known to cross the Amazon.' This is a classic country-specific field guide, respectfully observant of national boundaries.

By contrast, the 1954 European guide covered many countries, all Europe west of the 30° line of longitude, thus concerning itself with '452 basic species' and describing briefly 113 species listed as 'accidentals' that had been recorded in Europe less than 20 times. Later 'European' guides covered a wider area, such as the *1995 Collins Pocket Guide* that covered 'every species found regularly in Europe, North Africa and the Middle East'. That approach was influenced by the coverage of the nine-volume *Birds of the Western Palearctic* (1977–1994) that observed a complicated boundary drawn by reference to scholarly views and decisions to include or exclude certain habitat areas.

There is therefore an overlap between European guides that cover European Russia and *A Field Guide to the Birds of the USSR* (English edition, Princeton, 1984), covering 728 species in a vast area stretching east to the tip of Siberia, just opposite Alaska, and to the Kurile Islands, claimed also by Japan. That guide has been reprinted as *A Field Guide to Birds of Russia and Adjacent Territories*, an ominous sign for the independent countries described as 'Adjacent Territories'. Since publication, Russia has annexed part of Georgia, and the Crimea, and invaded Ukraine. This is another illustration that national boundaries can be an uncertain basis for a regional bird book. Geographic regions are more stable.

In 1987, while browsing in the bookshop of the American Museum of Natural History, New York, I was delighted to find that, at last, a field guide to New Guinea birds had been published: *Birds of New Guinea* (1986) by Beehler, Pratt and Zimmerman. The area covered was the large island of New Guinea, and 'West Papuan' and 'Eastern Papuan' islands, and some other small nearby islands. It therefore covered most of Papua New Guinea and part of Indonesia, but not the large islands of New Britain, New Ireland, Manus and Bougainville that are part of PNG. In his two-volume *Birds of Papua New Guinea* (1985, 1990 – not a field guide), Brian Coates had taken a different approach in including all of PNG: 'I have chosen political boundaries to delineate the area covered by this work because I believe every nation should have its own bird book.' However, a subsequent photographic guide (2001) extends the coverage to the whole island of New Guinea.

There is a revised edition of the Beehler guide continuing the same geographic coverage as previously: *Birds of New Guinea* (2015) by Thane Pratt and Bruce Beehler. It now covers 779 species, 70 more than the first edition. Yet another guide is *Birds of New Guinea including Bismarck Archipelago and Bougainville* (2017) by Phil Gregory, with the increased coverage as indicated by the title. Both those more recent field guides have taken up new taxonomic arrangements based on genetic data. Several new endemic songbird families have been created including the *Cnemophilidae* ('Satinbirds'), that bird photographed by Loke Wan Tho now being the 'Crested Satinbird'. 'Macgregor's Bird of Paradise' *Macgregoria pulchra* is now regarded as a honeyeater, variously labelled 'Macgregor's Honeyeater' and 'Giant Wattled Honeyeater'.

I expect that few people will be interested to learn that the most embracing of these recent books leaves out three fragments of PNG territory: (a) Takuu (Mortlock) Islands and (b) Nukumanu (Tasman) Islands (respectively 250 km and 520 km east from the northern tip of Bougainville), and (c) Pocklington Reef Island in the Coral Sea. Whether inclusion of those remote fragments with their marine spaces would add any oceanic seabirds or windblown strays to the New Guinea bird list I am unable to say. Probably no-one can say. Those tiny islets generate extensive areas of PNG sea areas, given 200-nautical-mile jurisdictional zones. Curiously, the Pratt/Beehler guide adopts a 200 km limit. The related Beehler/Pratt book (2016) restricts itself to seabirds 'within ca. 50 km of the mainland coastline and ca. 25 km of any fringing New Guinea island'. In fact, the whole Bismarck Sea is PNG territory by reason of archipelagic status.

The meaning of 'Australia' for field guide purposes has expanded, and therefore also, I assume, for most listers. Earlier books, the 1926 *Checklist* and the first Pizzey edition in 1980, for example, were limited to continental Australia, Tasmania and some nearby islands. In 1984, RAOU set the scene for expanded national species-ticking by publishing the first Christidis and Boles list, *The Taxonomy and Species of Birds of Australia and Its Territories*. This, and the 2008 list by the same authors, enlarged the coverage to 'island territories'. There was some looseness of language here, because at all relevant times Lord Howe Island was part of New South Wales, Macquarie Island was part of Tasmania, and the 'islands of Torres Strait' covered Queensland islands running from near the Australian mainland up to the coast of New Guinea. Saibai is as much part of Queensland as Moreton Island.

The Birdlife Australia Rarities Committee gives an appropriate description of the scope of an Australian bird list by referring to all external territories, thus including the often-forgotten Coral Sea Islands. Its task is:

> …maintaining a list of rare birds recorded in Australia and its external territories. This includes areas at sea that are within the exclusive economic zone, which is 200 nautical miles offshore or to agreed international boundaries such as those with Papua New Guinea, Timor and Indonesia.

The *Australian Bird Guide* has a useful map showing its own similar coverage. However, it fails to show those northernmost Queensland islands as caught by the Australian boundary.

Of course, you can forget about geographical boundaries and simply tick the birds listed in a particular book. Your list could include all the birds in one of those extended European field guides, or in a multi-country guide like *Birds of the Middle East* (1996), by Porter, Christensen and Schiermacker-Hansen. You could tick the birds it contains, separately, according to which country you were in whether that be Yemen, Jordan or Qatar. One would expect that in that part of the world you would be careful to keep in mind which country you were in at any particular moment. I see that *Birds of the Middle East* says you should 'consult a national avifauna' to learn the status of a species in any particular country. That is an easy matter today. On your computer you can go to *Avibase – Bird Checklists of the World*, and selecting, say, Bahrain, find that that country (780 sq km, one-third the area of the ACT) has a list, readily available, of 359 bird species. You would not find them all there on one day, though.

Avibase is setting a good example in taking us back to the proper meaning of 'checklist', that is a list of items needed, or things to be done. A field guide is one thing, a taxonomic list is another, and a checklist is yet another. I like the common-sense approach in *A Field Guide to the Birds of Hawaii and the Tropical Pacific* (1987) by H. Douglas Pratt, Bruner and Berrett. This contains six checklists for each Pacific island region in tabular form, each being divided into birds found in the constituent islands or small groups – 48 'checklists' in total. By the time you get down to Easter Island (Rapa) there are few land birds, although you might come across the Rapa Fruit-Dove. The authors suggest that you use the index as a 'master checklist'.

As mentioned, to some people field guides are, or were, collectable items because, taken together, they could provide a near-complete set of pictures of the bird species of the world. To me, so-called 'birds of the world' books were disappointing, offering only a very incomplete selection. However, a good effort was the 3,042-page *Birds of the World* edited by John Gooders. This was published in magazine form for binding, over 108 weeks in 1969–1971. By my count, there were about 150 contributors to the text. It was of uneven quality, but sometimes of expert standard. In the space available, it would be difficult to improve on the account of two New Guinea myna species, or the superb illustrations of them by Ken Lilly (page 2765). In that issue, the Starling was covered by Clive Minton, later famous in Australia as a shorebird expert. Towards the end of the series came short biographies of 'great bird artists' and a select list of 'bird books of the world'. There were short articles on hybrids, zoogeography (by Allan Keast), mapping populations, photographing birds (by Eric Hosking) and recording bird sounds (with a photo of the famous early recorder, Ludwig Koch, and his disc-cutting equipment).

However, the days of annoyingly incomplete world-bird-books were to end. In 1987, a Barcelona-based publishing firm, Lynx Edicions, was formed with a *Handbook of the Birds of the World* as its 'main target'. 'Ten large, weighty tomes' were envisaged. The aim was to fill gaps in the existing coverage by regional bird books. It was decided not to illustrate juvenile or immature or non-breeding plumages. Therefore, the work would not claim to be 'a sort of mammoth field guide'. Although in that sense the final product might be incomplete, it would be complete enough for me, so far as world-bird pictures were concerned. The final product, published from 1992 to 2013, ran to 16 volumes, all weighty as promised, plus a 'special volume'.

Lynx went on to join with the Cambridge-based Birdlife International to produce the two-volume *Illustrated Checklist of the Birds of the World* (2014, 2016). This, it was claimed, 'provided a profound taxonomic review of the previous publication'. At the present time, that *Checklist* remains the basis of the *Working List* used by Birdlife Australia. A third project has now been completed to serve 'a wider audience'. This is *All the Birds of the World* (2020). I would be inclined to classify this as a 'pictures' book, except for the amount of information that is provided in compressed form. This includes an abbreviated code that tells you how each species is classified in other global lists, and a QR code that refers your device to the species account in the vast information holdings of the Cornell Laboratory.

Peacock in flight in a Canberra suburb.

A hybrid lorikeet (Musk x Rainbow), with parents; rare visit of a Regent Honeyeater to north Canberra; Swift Parrot feeding in street ironbark;   Sharp-tailed Sandpipers in Australia (rare in North America) 'rich golden-buff with a bright chestnut-red cap, one of the most beautiful sandpipers I had ever seen' (Ken Kaufman).

98

Uses of photography (1) - showing what birds eat.

Black-shouldered Kite with rat;
Red Wattlebird with sugar; Pied Currawong
with glass of water; Little Bittern with fish;
Bassian Thrush with earthworms

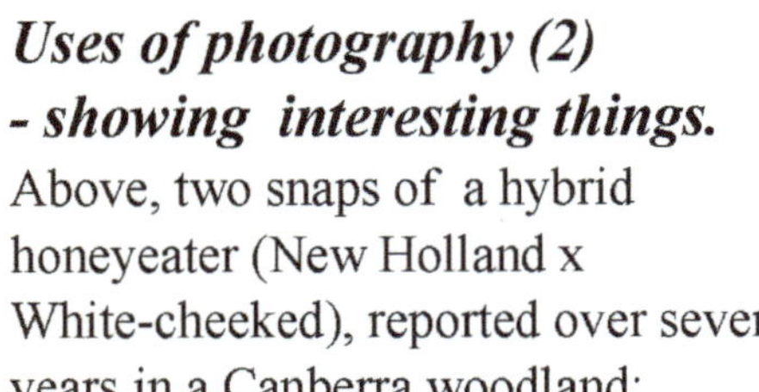

Uses of photography (2) - showing interesting things.

Above, two snaps of a hybrid honeyeater (New Holland x White-cheeked), reported over several years in a Canberra woodland; Eurasian Coot in unusual plumage.
Left, a much photographed suburban Powerful Owl, overhead with possum.
Right, Southern Boobook at least 16 years old, identified by photographing band at night.
Below, Emus walking on beach, Tuross Head.

Uses of photography (3) - showing identifying points of particular species.

As an example, the images shown here, published elsewhere, relate to members of the egret group : Great, Intermediate (or Plumed), Little, and Cattle. Field guides try to indicate such differences, but sometimes exaggerate them in doing so.   Moreover, field guides suffer from a lack of space to show everything that might be relevant. This group can sometimes be difficult because of seasonal variations.
(The egret B1 shown with 'cattle' is not a Cattle Egret.)

The wily Common Myna has developed strategies to resist attempts to eradicate it.

XVI

The English names of birds

At present the names given by classifiers are often an offence. A few evenings ago, I was charmed with an unaccustomed song coming out of a big pittosporum tree in my garden at Kew. I took careful note of the little warbler, and then consulted Mr Leach's *Descriptive List.* Judge of my satisfaction when I found that my little friend was "The Striated Field Wren or Stink Bird"!

–Frank Tate, Victorian Director of Education, 1911.

This, to me, is an important subject, although I will understand if most people don't think so. I must proceed carefully to avoid turning what seems a slightly dull subject into a totally boring one. Some names of Australian birds seem to be obscure or unjustifiably long. Consider the 11-year-old clutching his *What Bird is That?* ('the Cayley'), among a family of bird agnostics.

Grown-up: What's the name of that bird?

Child: It's a Black-faced Cuckoo-shrike.

Grown-up: Har, har. What does he think it is? Say that again. (*Everyone laughs*)

That sort of thing leads to reluctance to tell anyone a 'correct' bird name when your audience is not really interested. The fact is that many English names of Australian birds, while in a sense part of the language, are, in general, not part of ordinary speech. My father used to say 'laughing johnny' and 'mountain lory', probably names remembered from his childhood. Those names were part of ordinary speech. It is 'magpie', rather than 'Australian Magpie' that is in general use. People say 'seagull', with 'Silver Gull' rarely heard in ordinary speech. On the other hand, 'willie wagtail' is acceptable. Everyone says 'willie wagtail'.

The Cayley used the English names settled on in the 1926 *Checklist*. There is some of the background to that in the Libby Robin book. In the 1970s, the whole Australian list of English names was reconsidered under the authority of the RAOU. That was when

'Masked Lapwing' replaced 'Spur-winged Plover', and new spellings like 'Glossy Black-Cockatoo' were introduced. The new names were used in the Christidis and Boles lists in 1994 and 2008.

If you want an account of all the English names that have been used for Australian birds you will find it in *Australian Bird Names: Origins and Meanings* (2013, 2nd ed. 2019), by Ian Fraser and Jeannie Gray.

Roy Mackay writing about Port Moresby birds in 1969, had a problem in finding appropriate 'common names'. 'Each author who has used them for New Guinea birds gives a different name for each species, and as a result, there is some confusion.' He used the American-invented 'Black-faced Greybird' for the Black-faced Cuckoo-shrike ('Black-faced Cuckooshrike' in Cayley). Various approaches have been taken by authors who need to give English names to species that have no established English name. Often, they just make them up.

There is a relatively new book, *Birds of the Indonesian Archipelago* (2016), by James Eaton and three others. This covers Timor and other parts of 'Wallacea' and hence includes some Australian birds. The authors notify their intention to change some 'English group names', these being usually the noun in a bird name. This leads to 'Willie Fantail'. Odd-sounding though it is, the authors have a point. In Indonesia, the Willie sits in a single genus containing 22 other 'Fantails'. From the viewpoint of the northern hemisphere a 'Wagtail' is something quite different.

So, there is much room for differences of opinion. You only need two people together for a disagreement about names to emerge. When Charles Sibley and Burt Monroe wrote *Distribution and Taxonomy of Birds of the World* they covered 9,762 species, and were presumably in agreement about those. Not so much with regard to the English names. Sibley wrote in the introduction:

> Burt also organized a world-wide correspondence group to provide input and exchange of ideas on English names. Since this may turn out to be one of the most controversial features, I refer critics to Burt. I had little to do with this aspect – may even be one of the critics.

In the 1990s, Simon Bennett was offering a digital record-keeping program called 'Birdinfo'. I got this from him not to tick birds but to keep track of my accumulation of published bird pictures. Simon had based his program on the checklist developed by James Clements. (That list, much used by American birdians, was later taken over by Cornell Lab, which continues to update it.) Simon was a member of a Birds Australia committee advising on English names for the Australian list, and he was responsible for my joining it, in 2010. At that time, the list was the one in Christidis and Boles (2008). Both Les and Walter were on the committee. In view of the effort taken to settle English names, including a 1994 poll in which 1,300 people had voted, the committee was required to adopt a conservative policy in considering any changes. The committee is referred to here as 'ENC' – for 'English Names Committee'.

There was uncertainty about how the list would be updated to keep up with taxonomic changes. Other lists had emerged, in the form of global lists, such as eBird (maintained by Cornell Lab) and a list referred to as 'IOC', originally associated with the International Ornithologists' Union. Christidis and Boles (2008) is still there to be used, although it has not been updated. Birdlife Australia decided to add to these by adopting another list, for its own projects. This is known as the 'Working List of Australian Birds'. So far as taxonomic choices are concerned, it is based on the global list used by Birdlife International, a conservation organisation based in Cambridge, UK. Birdlife Australia does not make taxonomic decisions affecting species in the Working List.

In 2015, the chair of the ENC became vacant and I volunteered to take it on. There has not been a lot of work so far as new species are concerned. If a new species arrives in Australia and is accepted by the Rarities Committee, it is usually given the English name by which it is known in international usage or in the place it comes from. A few other changes have been made, for example: 'Australian Painted-snipe' instead of 'Australian Painted Snipe' (because it is not really a snipe); 'Mallard' instead of 'Northern Mallard' (because there is only one Mallard species); 'Green Oriole' instead of 'Yellow Oriole' (as more accurate, and to follow global practice). Among current issues is whether to adopt, for example, 'Scarlet Myzomela' instead of 'Scarlet Honeyeater', the reason being the practice in global lists.

The ENC reports to a committee with general oversight in the Birdlife Australia structure. There have been exchanges between the two committees about moving away from the 'conservative principle' and making more widespread changes to English names that are seen as unsatisfactory for one reason or other. For example, there are complaints about 'Major Mitchell's Cockatoo' which is named for an explorer associated with violent acts against aboriginal people on one of his expeditions. Some people point to research suggesting that a mere name can create negative feelings about a bird even if nothing is known about the bird itself. Although it is not an Australian bird, 'Spiny Babbler' would be one of those, because both spines and babbling are unattractive qualities, and the bird, as we now know, is not even rare. As you can imagine, people have different views about what is a sufficient reason to change a name.

Another issue is whether more indigenous names should be used, bearing in mind the 'successful example of Budgerigar'. (Penny Olsen has referred me to respectable authority that 'Budgerigar' does not come from an aboriginal language. It is a compound word, largely of European construction, taking in a word like 'bedga', meaning 'good'.) That is part of a larger issue about using distinctive Australian names versus conforming with international practice. Sometimes there is an international reason that governs choice of name for an Australian species. There was a widespread species known as 'Gull-billed Tern', which was found in Australia. When the Australian subspecies was recognized as a separate species, an appropriate name for it was 'Australian Gull-billed Tern'. (Although it must be acknowledged that long names like that do annoy some people.) However, one global list rejected that choice and has invented the name 'Australian Tern'. Their reasoning is that if they accept 'Australian Gull-billed Tern' they will have to add an adjective (like 'Common') in front of 'Gull-billed Tern' to be used for the species outside Australia, which will mean an unnecessary name-change in a lot of other countries, not to mention the length of the name.

Because the Birdlife Australia Working List (WLAB) is only one of several lists that a bird observer might use, it does not have the same authority as the 1926 RAOU *Checklist* had in its time. However, the English names in it are those in reasonably common use. If you are using eBird you can select 'English (Australia)' from 15 versions of English names, and that will usually, but not always, give you the WLAB English name. The popular *Australian Bird Guide* (rev. ed. 2019) by Peter Menkhorst and others, follows the taxonomy in the IOC list rather than the BLI list, but generally uses the WLAB English name.

That might be enough about the contentious subject of English names for bird species. However, I do have to say something about subspecies.

Some name issues considered by the English Names Committee

Left, the 'Australian Gull-billed Tern' , but some prefer 'Australian Gull' for international reasons. Right, logic suggests 'Great Pied Cormorant', given there is a 'Little Pied Cormorant'.

In the Australian list, subspecies are given English names.   The three godwit subspecies have names according to their breeding areas. The one that visits eastern Australia (*Limosa lapponica baueri*) is called 'Alaskan Bar-tailed Godwit'.

Above, now 'Australian Painted-snipe', because it is not a snipe.

Right, Gould's 'Adelaide Rosella' is now regarded as an intermediate form between subspecies of Crimson Rosella. The name would be useful if agreement could be reached on the type or types referred to. (Two photos are by Greg Dare.)

The problem of agreeing on uniform English names.

The North American species on the left is known as 'Wood Duck', the name used by Audubon.   Gould used 'Maned Goose' for the above species, noting that 'Wood Duck' was sometimes use by 'the colonists'. The official name adopted in Australia in 1994 was 'Australian Wood Duck'. 'Maned Duck' is preferred by some, the only true 'Wood Duck' being the North American species.

'Maned Duck' has some attraction by reason of the appearance of the male (below).

Another 'international name' not popular in Australia is 'Myzomela' for some small honeyeaters that occur mainly outside Australia.

XVII

The world of subspecies

Despite the utility of delimiting subspecies, we guess that as many as half the currently accepted subspecies on earth listed in contemporary world checklists are poorly or very thinly defined and without true merit.

–Beehler and Pratt,
Birds of New Guinea: Distribution, Taxonomy and Systematics (2016)

In 1999, Dick Schodde and Ian Mason wrote that subspecies were the real units of diversity in birds and that many more subspecies were rare and endangered than 'biological species'. They complained that 'many fauna managers and birdwatchers' did not value them at the same level as species and some did 'not take them seriously at all'. (That was in the introduction to their ground-breaking catalogue, *Directory of Australian Birds: Passerines*. A second volume dealing with non-passerines is still awaited.) Today, I am sure that many more people do take subspecies seriously. Their status is dealt with in the national assessment published every 10 years as *The Action Plan for Australian Birds*, principal author Stephen Garnett. Where appropriate, they are covered in Commonwealth and State/Territory conservation legislation.

The new importance of subspecies has given rise to some interesting English name issues. Birdlife Australia took the unusual step of assigning an English name to *each* subspecies on its list. That step had been rejected in 1978, but in 2012, with increasing interest in subspecies, especially for conservation, it was believed a standard subspecies name would help inform the Australian public, and would be useful in legislation. Are English names for subspecies a good idea? When this comes up, people talk about the name, 'Helmeted Honeyeater', a critically endangered subspecies that is the bird emblem of Victoria. The name 'Helmeted Honeyeater' can be called a success. It is fairly short, easily remembered, widely known. It is a subspecies rather than a full species, but if that is important to someone they will almost certainly know that it is 'only' a subspecies.

The problem is that inventing new English names for all subspecies is likely to create confusion about what the new name refers to when it is detached from the scientific name.

For example, what is a 'South-eastern Boobook'? In most of the new English names that uncertainty is met by taking the species name and adding before it a geographical description. Thus, 'Cape York Rufous Owl' refers to the subspecies of the Rufous Owl that is found in Cape York. However, many names are not as clear as that. Moreover, some are so long and awkward that people are unlikely to use them, such as 'Northern Australian Yellow White-eye'. To be consistent, 'South-eastern Boobook' should be 'South-eastern Southern Boobook', but that sounds very awkward.

As the English names for subspecies are not widely used, most of the present names can be regarded as provisional until a better name is proposed. For example, for a threatened species, a particular new name might be regarded as best for the purpose of a recovery program.

The following is an example of a recent name-selection issue. Andrew Black, a member of ENC and a grasswren authority, had already published, with Peter Gower, their *Grasswrens - Australian outback identities* (2017). A proposed revision of the Striated Grasswren complex was awaiting publication in *Emu*. Instead of one species with three subspecies, the new arrangement called for three species and seven subspecies. Four of the subspecies are threatened. Able to consider English names before publication and adoption in any global list, ENC could endorse Andrew's preferred names for the new species: 'Rufous Grasswren' *A. whitei* and 'Opalton Grasswren' *A. rowleyi*. For the two subspecies remaining in *A. striatus*, Andrew favoured 'Eastern Striated Grasswren' *A. s. striatus* and 'Murray Mallee Striated Grasswren' *A. s. howei*. Strong representations were received for *A. s. striatus*, in view of the location of its tiny range, to be given an aboriginal name, but no name was suggested at the time. The English *species* names have been followed in the IOC list.

Soon after, Mick Todd, an officer with the NSW environment department, after consultation with traditional owners in the area, proposed for *A. s. striatus* the name Mukarrthippi (= 'spinifex bird') Grasswren. This was adopted, and Birdlife Australia applauded the name as a NAIDOC week initiative. 'The hope is that this beautiful new name will inspire re-doubled conservation efforts'. As it is a subspecies name, it will not have to pass a test of acceptability by global lists, which do not give English names for subspecies.

However, there are signs that the Cornell Lab enterprise, which includes eBird, is going to give more attention to subspecies. Already it is possible to tick in eBird 'Varied Sittella

(Orange-winged)' and 'Crested Shrike-tit (Eastern)'. Perhaps one day you will be able to tick 'Striated Grasswren (Mukarrthippi)'.

The ENC became involved in the search for the Adelaide Rosella. This is not the usual kind of quest, like looking for the Pink-headed Duck. An Adelaide Rosella is what I believe the philosophers might call 'a construct'. There are several possible Adelaide Rosellas, but which is the true one?

The bird, named by Gould, was seen alive and well in the pages of Joe Forshaw's *Australian Parrots* (rev. ed. 1981). In William Cooper's painting, two 'Adelaide Rosellas' were shown together, the variable but generally reddish *P. a. adelaidae* and the paler orange-yellow *subadelaidae*. The species was still alive, with the same two subspecies, in *Handbook of the Birds of the World* (HBW) vol. 4 (1997).

In 2014, along came a new *Checklist* jointly produced by HBW and Birdlife International, which Birdlife Australia takes as its guiding authority. The Crimson Rosella *P. elegans* is regarded as containing seven subspecies, including *subadelaidae,* and *fleurieuensis*. '*Adelaidae*' is no longer referred to as a species or subspecies, being regarded as an intergrade between *subadelaidae* and *fleurieuensis*. That arrangement is quite respectable, being based on work in CSIRO, and followed also in the IOC list. It is also followed in Birdlife Australia's Working List.

However, the English name 'Adelaide Rosella' had disappeared. In October 2016, the English Names Committee considered there was a strong case for making use of the still widely used name 'Adelaide Rosella' for the intergradient population. A recommendation to that effect was accepted. In WLAB version two, so the following name appeared: 'Adelaide Rosella *P.e. fleurieuensis x P. e. subadelaidae*'. Without explanation, that name has disappeared from version three.

Nonetheless, people are still finding an Adelaide Rosella to tick. The *Australian Bird Guide* tells you that 'Adelaide Rosella' (or 'Adelaide Rosellas') refers to subspecies *subadelaidae* and *fleurieuensis* and their hybrids. If using eBird, you will find it recognizes 'Crimson Rosella (Adelaide) *Platycercus elegans adelaidae/subadelaidae*'. It appears from the parent Cornell Lab site that 'Crimson Rosella (Adelaide)' refers to the two subspecies recognized by Forshaw and HBW, although the relevant species is now *P. elegans*, rather than *P. adelaidae*. According to Cornell Lab, it is *P. e. fleurieuensis* that has disappeared.

XVIII

The New Guinea connection, again

This story begins with a photographic incident. In September 2011, I drove to northern NSW to stay with some friends on their newly acquired farmlet near Dorrigo. On the way back, I used campgrounds along the coast, staying a night or two at each. One of these was at Kylie's Beach, named, I found, for the famous author Kylie Tennant. Next morning on a walk along the scenic beach I came across a family of Red-backed Fairy-wrens, a species that must have been near its southern limit at that point. I took a few snaps of the male. At that time I had been putting occasional videos and an odd snap or two on a website maintained by the Lynx Edicions people under the name 'Internet Bird Collection'. (It has since been taken over by Cornell Lab, but I haven't got around to transferring over any of my material.) The Kylie's fairy-wrens must have been on display because I had a call from a book editor who wanted to use a photo of one 'on a book cover'. They offered me a few copies of the book.

That was how (a) I came to acquire several copies of *Where Song Began* and (b) a small photo of the R-b Fairy-wren came to appear on the back cover of the first printing, although I don't know why the species was chosen. Now, about Tim Low's much-publicised 2014 book. There is so much information in it that it is hard to give a summary. It is about Australia's native bird species, their classification and their biology, and things that make them different from birds elsewhere. I have heard Tim Low say of the book at a later interview:

The Red-backed Fairy-wren photographed at Kylie's Beach.

'Writing a book is storytelling – you've got to entertain' (Adelaide Writers' Week, 2015.) Reading this one, you can see what he means. Nonetheless, it seems to me to be written with some authority, sprinkled liberally with sources and quoting the appropriate people. The interesting part about the northern hemisphere's songbirds originating in Australia (meaning that an ancestor songbird came from Australia) might be the most important part, but takes up a bit more than one chapter.

The part about Australia and New Guinea forming a single bird region reflects a theme now heard more often. According to Low, biologically speaking, 'the island is not so much a neighbour of Australia as a core part of it'. This gives rise to some awkwardness when he says that from the New Guinea chapter (Chapter 4) 'when I say "Australia" I have New Guinea (with Papua) in mind as well'. Pratt and Beehler (in *Birds of New Guinea* (2016) – the companion to the field guide) say 'New Guinea and Australia share the Australian plate … New Guinea is the high, wet and equatorial sector, whereas continental Australia is the low, dry and temperate sector'. However, from the viewpoint of the bird-seeking tourist, the two 'sectors' are very different from one another, as regards topography, culture and social conditions. I do not know if a Big Year has been attempted in PNG, but no book about one is yet available. If one appears, a mere documentary will not do it justice. A full-length movie will be required.

It seems there is much still to be learnt about New Guinea's birds, and how they fit into the broader story of bird evolution. That is my conclusion after looking into yet another book: *The Largest Avian Radiation, The Evolution of Perching Birds, or the Order Passeriformes* (2020), by John Fjeldsa, Les Christidis and Per Ericson (editors). This book offers the latest information about relationships, based on molecular studies. The editors accept that songbirds ('oscine passerines') originated 'down under'. However, it is now suggested that New Guinea rather than Australia was the source. Australia had the oldest oscine groups 'but exported few of them'. Although not universally agreed, according to the theory now advanced, New Guinea (or emerging islands where New Guinea is now) was 'a cradle of two slightly younger radiations that colonized other parts of the world'. Three relevant groupings are recognized:

1) 'Basal oscine families': e.g., treecreepers, bowerbirds, fairy-wrens, thornbills, honeyeaters. These are mainly known from Australia and New Guinea.

2) The 'crow-like passerines' (parvorder Corvida): e.g., crows, Australian magpies, whistlers, shrikes, cuckoo-shrikes, birds of paradise. Highest diversity is found

on the island of New Guinea. '[W]e assume that this is where the group originated … when coral platforms in the epicontinental seas north of Australia began to emerge above sea level'.

3) The 'higher songbirds', the *Passerida* group, now represented by some 3,800 species, 'apparently originated after a single dispersal from the Australasian area (or, most likely, from New Guinea) to the Old World'. This great branch includes the superfamilies – *Paroidea* (tits, chickadees), *Sylvioidea* (Old World warblers, larks, grassbirds, swallows, white-eyes), *Muscicapoidea* (starlings, old world flycatchers, thrushes), *Passeroidea* (sunbirds, weaverbirds, grass-finches, pipits, finches, new world warblers).

So, a large part of the history of birds comes back to New Guinea. As the crusty Charles Monckton, FRGS, FGS, FRAI, wrote in 1922:

Any enterprising young man, with a taste for natural history and a small private income, has yet to find in New Guinea fauna a rich field in which he may build for himself an undying monument. I know of no other country in the world offering such an opportunity to the enterprising.

(I should add that that one editor of the *Largest Avian Radiation*, Les Christidis, still prefers an Australian rather than New Guinea origin for the relevant radiation.)

Two 'Australo-Papuan Robins' from Gould/Sharpe, *Birds of New Guinea and Adjacent Islands*. Their ancestors might have taken flight from their island home to become the foundation of a great limb of the avian tree.

Creators of recent bird books.

Prolific bird-book author Penny Olsen at her work station in the National Library of Australia. On shelf behind is a copy of *Cayley & Son*. Nature writer Ian Fraser was a member of a keen band of self-confessed twitchers. Some of them are below watching a painted-snipe. Ian wears the claret shirt and beard. He co-authored the invaluable reference *Australian Bird Names*.

Below. Ian Mason, co-author of *Passions in Ornithology*, the comprehensive account of egg-collecting in Australia. He is measuring Brolga eggs in the Australian National Wildlife Collection.

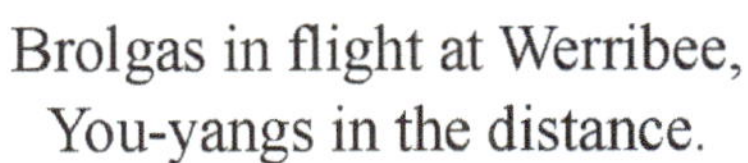

Brolgas in flight at Werribee, You-yangs in the distance.

Two avian taxonomists. The influential Nigel Collar supports the approach taken by BirdLife International and BirdLife Australia. He was good enough to pose with Serin and Raile, all being Cambridge residents. (2021 photo)
Below, Dick Schodde works on a collection of cockatoo skulls in Australian National Wildlife Collection (2015).

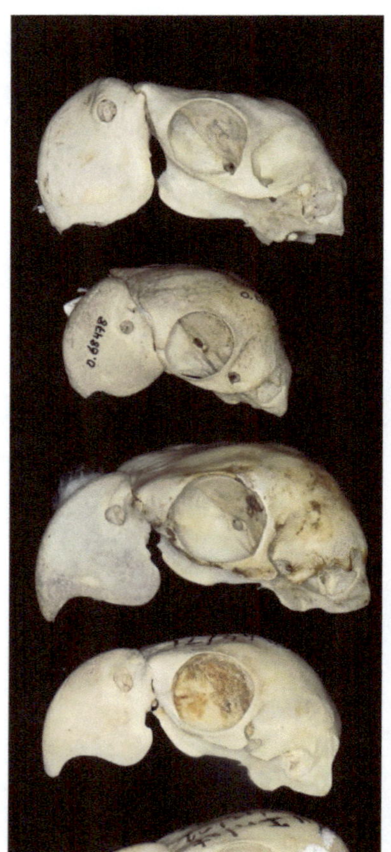

The importance of
New Guinea, yet
again. Leo Joseph
with helpful maps
displayed for
reference in the
Australian
National Wildlife
Collection.

Below, Leo discusses a diagram indicating genetic differences between subspecies of
Forest Kingfisher in New Guinea. One is resident, one a migrant from Australia. The row
of specimens near Leo was collected in the Port Moresby area.

A row of White-fronted Chats is at lower right.

117

XIX

On the trail of the Mock Ibis and the Bin Chicken

William Golding, the celebrated English author who wrote *Lord of the Flies* (1954), and won a Nobel Prize for Literature, also wrote a travel book, *An Egyptian Journal* (1985). That book was about a leisurely boat trip up the Nile. It contains some scattered observations about bird life along the river.

Here is one observation, made at a flooded field:

> There were a few large, white birds picking about in the water and on the banks. They were the *Amis des Paysans*, or mock ibis, the Farmer's Friends. I asked about them … and found that they are decreasing in numbers because of the build-up of insecticides.

The large white birds must have been Cattle Egrets, which occur in some numbers at places along the Nile valley. But why 'mock ibis'? There is a curious story about the confusion of two species.

The 'ibis' that was sacred in ancient Egypt, and known as 'ibis' to the Greeks and Romans, disappeared from Egypt, probably well before the 18th century brought an emerging curiosity about the natural world. Linnaeus, the Swedish naturalist who devised the naming system used today, believed that the ancient authors who spoke of 'ibis' were referring to the Cattle Egret, then common in Egypt. In 1757, Linnaeus gave the specific name *ibis* to the egret. In English, the egret was sometimes referred to as 'Egyptian Ibis'.

In Victorian and Edwardian times, Egypt was a favourite destination for wealthy sightseers and sojourners from Europe. Such was the interest in Egypt's antiquities and other curiosities that the artist Charles Whymper (1853–1941) produced a book for such visitors: *Egyptian Birds – for the most part seen in the Nile Valley* (1909).

Although he had reservations about including the absent 'Sacred Ibis' in the book, he gave two reasons for doing so.

118

> The first is, that from one cause or another the Sacred Ibis is a bird so wrapped up with all our ideas of Egypt, and almost representative of the birds of Egypt, that most, although they do not know the bird, are interested in its existence. The second is one that follows this known interest, namely exposing of the dragoman's oft-repeated lie, that he can, and does, show the newcomer Sacred Ibises, whereas he cannot and does not.

(At the time, in some eastern Mediterranean countries, 'dragoman' was a common name for an interpreter or guide.)

With respect to the 'Buff-backed Egret', now known as the Cattle Egret, Whymper said:

> The Egret is one of the many birds that the dragoman makes the tourist happy by calling 'the Ibis', and the number that return to their friends gleefully telling how they saw a flock of Ibises grows every season. In the article on the Ibis I have shown how ludicrously untrustworthy is the dragoman's Natural History information.

The 'article on the Ibis' read, in part:

> Time after time I have been solemnly informed that four or five, or a round dozen, Ibises had been seen at such and such a place. On inquiry I have been told there could be no mistake, as dear So-and-so, the dragoman, had pointed them out and assured all and sundry that they were 'genuine Sacred Ibis'. And though strange, it is true, people prefer to believe a lie if it confirms what they wish, than the truth if it does not. The sad truth is there are no Sacred Ibises in Egypt at all …

If it seems strange that persons interested in birds could be misled by such wrong ID advice, remember that 'the field guide in the modern sense' did not exist 100 years ago.

Despite Whymper's indignation, there is some evidence that in 19th century Egypt *the egret was* 'the sacred ibis' in common, if careless, usage. One author writes of the contemporary traveler meeting with 'the sacred ibis, the typical bird of Egypt', then describes its behaviour (being clearly that of the egret), then goes on 'what is called the sacred ibis seems to be really identical with the buff-backed heron'. The reason is that '*Ibis religiosa* … if once an inhabitant of Egypt, is no longer found there, except in a mummified state in the pits of Memphis and Thebes'. (Adams, 1880).

Another 19th century writer accepts that 'Ibis aethiopica' is the sacred ibis of the ancient Egyptians but quotes another as pointing out that the buff-backed heron 'does duty on the Nile as the ibis, being generally pointed out to travelers by dragomans, etc., as the real *Ibis religiosa*.' (Kingsley ed., 1885)

From time to time, a similar species in Australia has been treated as the same species as the bird once known in Egypt. In a talk at Moree (western NSW) on Australian birds, Neville Cayley:

> …said the ibis was worshipped by Egyptians, and should be worshipped in Australia. It was one of the means by which liver fluke in sheep could be kept down. The bird ate fresh water snails, which were the host of the liver fluke. (*Warialda Standard and Northern Districts' Advertiser* (NSW) 6 November 1933)

By 1989, the 'Sacred Ibis *Theskiornis aethiopica*' was reported to be at home in central Sydney. 'They have been nesting in the Zoo grounds for a number of years and have extended their range to the Botanic Gardens and Centennial Park, where they breed, and other locations close to Sydney Harbour.' (Hoskin)

Confirmed as a separate species in 1994, the White Ibis celebrated by exploding in greater numbers from its rural wetlands and becoming an ever-more-intrusive urban scavenger in many towns of eastern Australia. I remember a not unusual experience at a café in the Sydney botanic gardens when an ibis mounted the table and took food from my plate. It is often seen foraging at garbage landfills.

One authority has recorded 'Bin Chicken', 'Sandwich Snatcher' and 'Tip Turkey' among 13 new names that refer to that kind of behaviour. The ibis is said to have 'achieved a spectacular media, and especially social media, presence'. In 2017, in a poll run by a newspaper and Birdlife Australia, it came second for Australian Bird of the Year. (Fraser and Gray)

Even more surprisingly, it became a favourite subject for tattoos, particularly among visiting backpackers, as a souvenir more reminiscent of Australia than the kangaroo. Just put 'bin chicken tattoo' in your digital search engine. The height of that particular cult seems to have been around 2017. One reason for its notoriety, and popularity as a pictorial subject, is that it is easily recognisable. Moreover, as the ancient Egyptians knew, it is easy to draw.

Once again, the position with respect to an English name is not satisfactory. Birdlife International uses 'African Sacred Ibis' for the species formerly found in Egypt, and 'Australian Ibis' for the closely related species found in Australia. There are other species of ibis in Australia. BLI declines to follow the Australian name of 'Australian White Ibis' as there is another 'White Ibis', not closely related, in the Americas.

Given that the Australian species is at home in an urban setting, there is a question about the preferred habitat of the Egyptian counterpart. Whymper believed that it disappeared because it needed 'the great jungle-like brakes of papyrus that grow rampantly along the river course' to the south of Khartoum. (Whymper could only find some papyrus for his imaginative painting in the garden of a friend's house in upper Egypt.) On the other hand, Strabo, a Greek writer at about the time of Cleopatra, is quoted as reporting:

> Every street in Alexandria is full of them. In certain respects, they are useful, in others troublesome. They are useful because they pick up all sorts of small animals, and the offal thrown out of butchers' and cooks' shops. They are troublesome because they devour everything, are dirty, and with difficulty prevented from polluting in every way what is clean, and what is not given to them. (Quoted in Kingsley ed.)

That sounds like our Bin Chicken. As I write, it has been announced that Brisbane will hold the 2032 Olympic Games. Immediately some people are suggesting the Bin Chicken as the official mascot. Surely, the cult will have faded by then (?).

References relating to Chapter XIX:

Adams, W. H. D. and Giacomelli, H. *The Bird World* (1888) Thomas Nelson, London

Carey, J. *William Golding: The Man Who Wrote Lord of the Flies* (2009) Faber & Faber, London

Christidis, L. and Boles, W. *The Taxonomy and Species of Birds of Australia and its Territories* (1994) RAOU, Hawthorn East.

Golding, W. *Lord of the Flies* (1954) Faber & Faber, London.

Golding, W. *An Egyptian Journal* (1985) Faber & Faber, London

Goodman, S.M. and Meininger, P.L. (Eds.) *The Birds of Egypt* (1989) OUP, New York

Hosking, E. S. *The Birds of Sydney 1770-1989* (1991) Surrey Beatty, Chipping Norton, NSW

Fraser, I, and Gray, J. *Australian Bird Names* 2nd ed. (2019) CSIRO Publishing, Clayton South.

Kingsley, J. S. (Ed.) *The Riverside Natural History vol. IV Birds* (1888) Houghton Mifflin, Cambridge, Mass.

Marchant, S. and Higgins, P.J. (Coordinators) *Handbook of Australian, New Zealand & Antarctic Birds* (HANZAB) vol. I part B (1990) OUP, Melbourne.

Whymper, C. *Egyptian Birds* (1909) Adam and Charles Black, London.

Year of the Bin Chicken.   1. Charles Whymper's imaginary ibis at home in a papyrus swamp. 2.   An unusual Bin Chicken gives its views to a birdian, Kelly Swamp. 3. An ancient ibis in Egypt, from the Kingsley book.   4. A slightly discoloured example of the Australian relative, in a preening moment. 5.   A common sight in Canberra skies, a flock commuting between their roost and a landfill feeding spot.

XX

The popularity of science

Approaching the end of this brief survey of bird books of the world, I see a sub-category that needs its own short chapter. Typically, this is represented by a book by a professional writer that makes a story about changing perceptions and scientific discovery. *Where Song Began*, by Tim Low, is a good example. Another example is *The Beak of the Finch* (1994) by Jonathan Weiner. Although scientifically informed, these are written as popular books, not as contributions to science.

Weiner's book won a Pulitzer Prize in 1995 in General Nonfiction: 'For a distinguished book of non-fiction by an American author that is not eligible for consideration in any other category'. The book is about the evolution of finches in the Galapagos Islands. The citation quoted 'the jacket':

> But Darwin himself never saw evolution as Peter and Rosemary Grant have been seeing it – in the act of happening. For more than twenty years they have been monitoring generation after generation of finches on the island of Daphne Major ... And we watch the Grants' team observe evolution at a level that was totally inaccessible to Darwin: the molecular level, as the DNA in the blood samples taken from the birds reveals evolutionary change.

The point is that on those isolated islands only certain kinds of seeds are periodically available, according to climatic conditions from year to year. Finches with bills of the right size and shape to deal with them survive and breed. Others don't. Evolution happening, right there.

Another book in this sub-category is *The Lost Birds of Paradise* (1995) by Errol Fuller. This is about examples of birds of paradise that do not fit in to the existing recognized species. (Forty-three recognized species are suggested, but there are different opinions about that.) Nineteen 'lost' species are considered, these being presumed to be naturally occurring hybrids, or members of species that are extinct or awaiting rediscovery. One of these is *Paradisea mixta*, believed to be a hybrid between *P. minor* and *P. raggiana*. Existence of such a hybrid form had been confirmed by, among others, E. Thomas Gilliard.

123

However, Fuller's entry on this hybrid is largely given over to a discussion of the New Guinea exploits of, of all people, Errol Flynn, well-known Hollywood actor. The book to be noted here is Flynn's autobiography, *My Wicked, Wicked Ways* (1960), a book not claimed here to be in the popular science category.

Flynn is introduced into the story because in the course of his adventurous career he came to New Guinea just a few years after *P. mixta* was described, and set about making his fortune from the bird of paradise plumes trade. 'Just as *Paradisaea mixta*'s gracing of the list of legitimate species was destined to be short-lived (nine years), so too was Errol Flynn's flirtation with the birds of paradise and the natural history of New Guinea.'

As Flynn relates the story, he attempted to float down the Sepik River on a bamboo raft laden with all his possessions, including 'all of [his] bird of paradise carcasses, preserved in salt'. The raft was split apart on rocks. 'All of it was washed away, birds of paradise, feathers, plumage, salt and all'.

The book is still in the future, but many stories about the private lives of fairy-wrens have been told by Andrew Cockburn. His long-running research is based at the Australian National Botanic Gardens, Canberra. Andrew says that this individual (rnNB, banded 9 Jan 2009) 'has a fairly noble heritage. His mum (MybA) was sired by a 2006 male called weNG, who was a grandchild of a famous male called MnyG, and a great grandchild of the most famous female called BRN, via her most successful son NRY and the other most famous female called ORB via her son WBW'.

XXI

The mystery of the travelling snipe

The numbers in which they appear vary, the impression prevailing that of late years they have steadily decreased.
Doubtless the snipe is the king of all our sporting birds …
　　　　　　　　　　　–Charles Belcher, *The Birds of the District of Geelong, Australia* (1914)

Here is another book, *British Game* (1946) by Brian Vesey-Fitzgerald. Twelve pages are devoted to 'The Snipe'. The author says: 'You may find the common snipe almost anywhere in this country provided only that the ground is wet'. Not the kind of bird you would find in most of Australia then.

The National Library of Australia offers a digital research aid called 'Trove'. You can use this to search the contents of newspaper issues up to 1954. If you search for use of the word 'snipe', you will find reports, from a time now past, indicating a preoccupation with shooting the first snipe of the season. *Sydney Morning Herald*, 11 September 1900: 'The first snipe of the season within the suburban area was shot on Saturday at Pymble by [etc] …' The area near the later Canberra gets several mentions, for example: 'The first snipe of the season for this district – possibly for the Commonwealth – was bagged by Mr A. A. Payten at Towrang on Wednesday last …' (*Goulburn Evening Penny Post*, 4 October 1917, so a curiously late report for an unlikely claim).

One would expect serious snipe-shooters to have the identification right. However, it is difficult to be confident about the following report, evidently relating to more than one visiting species (*Geelong Advertiser*, 11 March 1851):

Myriads of snipe, more especially of sand snipe, are now swarming round and over the Lakes. Clouds of them may be seen at day break, rising from the smooth expanse of the water and sweeping in eccentric figures, looking at a distance like rime, or vapor driven about then breaking into parties, joining again, and disappearing in the flats. Large snipe, too, are getting plentiful, but are rather shy, they are in splendid condition, and a few dust shot well aimed would not be thrown away upon them. It is needless to add that they form a grateful dish at the breakfast table, and are very palatable roasted feathers and all in a bush fire …

The snipe species of south-eastern Australia is now known as Latham's (or Japanese) Snipe *Gallinago hardwickii*. Around Canberra it is fairly common, in the warmer months, at local wetlands. Over the years, I have taken thousands of photos of them, as well as some early digital video. I consult here volume 3 of the Lynx Edicions *Handbook*. I see that our species is of variable size but larger than the Common Snipe. It is 'extremely similar' to another snipe recorded in northern Australia (Swinhoe's (or Marsh) Snipe *G. megala*), but slightly larger. According to *Australian Bird Guide*, it has only 14–18 tail feathers compared to 24–28 for Swinhoe's. In New Guinea, where Swinhoe's is more common, the similarity of the two species has raised questions about past records.

Kelly Swamp is part of Canberra wetlands known as 'Jerra' (for 'Jerrabomberra'). The snipe-frequented area includes sewage ponds and a turf farm. At Kelly Swamp there are viewing shelters that draw observers to see waterbirds. In general, visiting species from the northern hemisphere are rarities. The snipe are an exception, a particular attraction by reason of their regular seasonal occurrence, and the fact that they 'come from Japan'.

In the little volume mentioned above as associated with Lord Alanbrooke, Prince Nobusuke Takatukasa writes that Latham's Snipe 'reminds one closely of the common snipe, but is much larger. In summer, it often soars and circles in the sky, drumming tremendously, with its tail-feathers spread out, and calling *"zeep, zeep"*'. That was for the information of the English-speaking foreigner visiting Japan in 1941.

The author of the Lynx *Handbook* entry (1996) says: 'Migration route is still a mystery; presumably flies from Japan to E. Australia in a few days, non-stop or stopping at only a few staging sites, e.g., New Guinea and N Australia'. The popular literature is not much help here. Pratt (1987) says that up till that date Latham's Snipe had been reported only once in the tropical Pacific, a single record from Kwajalein, Marshall Islands, about 2,500 km west of a direct route between eastern Australia and Japan. On the other hand, Swinhoe's Snipe is an 'uncommon migrant and rare winter resident in western Micronesia'. An earlier book on Micronesia, Baker (1951), does not mention Latham's Snipe at all. Latham's Snipe is described as 'Rare/Accidental' on Guam. (*Avibase*)

Ebird shows no records of Latham's Snipe on the sparse islands in the great expanse between New Guinea and Japan. There are three records in the New Guinea Highlands: single birds in 1986 (25 October), 1987 (29 September), and 2018 (24 October). The first two, typically for remote New Guinea sites, were at airfields.

Rand and Gilliard (1967) gives only two records for New Guinea. Both are interesting. The first was collected by Austin Rand on 27 August 1938 on the northern slopes of what was then Mount Wilhelmina, now in the Indonesian province of West Papua. The location was at an altitude of 3,550 metres. The second was in September 1951 in the Wahgi Valley, near Nondugl when that station was under the management of Nep Blood. Some authorities regard those as the only reliable records from the NG highlands, other (sight) records being uncertain by reason of possible confusion with Swinhoe's Snipe. (Bishop)

The Canberra snipe community (birds and humans) now has a part to play here. I owe the following information to Birgita Hansen, an organiser of the Latham's Snipe Project. In February 2019, a captured snipe, found to be large enough to carry a satellite transmitter, was released at Kelly Swamp. This was a female tagged as snipe 66. Last recorded at the sewage ponds on 8 March, she was near Mackay, north Queensland, on 13 April and in the PNG lowlands on 15 April. When last heard from, the transmitter had been for five days, up to 22 April, in Enga Province, about 30 km west of Wabag.

In 2020, tagged snipe 59 left the Jerra area at about the beginning of February. Its transmitter was last heard from over several days up to 10 May, in the vicinity of Koroba, in a valley in the PNG Southern Highlands Province. In a straight line that is about 85 km from the last transmission from snipe 66. We now know something about the line of the migration route of this species, but the typical pattern of movement is still a mystery. Does the northward movement typically involve a stay in New Guinea, or are delays there caused by weather or other adverse conditions? If some birds do not proceed further north than New Guinea, how often does that happen, and what is the reason?

Some references for Chapter XXI

Baker, R. H. *The Avifauna of Micronesia. Its Origin, Evolution and Distrib*ution (1951) University of Kansas, Lawrence.

Beehler, B. M. & Pratt, T. K. *Birds of New Guinea: Distribution, Taxonomy and Systematics* (2016). *Princeton.*

Bishop, K. D. 'Shorebirds in New Guinea: their status, conservation and distribution.' (2006) *Stilt* 50: 103–134.

Coates, B. J. *The Birds of Papua New Guinea*, vol. 1 Non-Passerines. Dove Publications, Alderley, Qld.

del Hoyo, J., Elliott, A. & Sargatal, J. (eds.) *Handbook of the Birds of the World*, vol. 3 Hoatzin to Auks. (1996) Lynx Edicions, Barcelona.

Hansen, B. D. & others. *Revision of the East Asian - Australasian Flyway Population Estimates for 37 Listed Migratory Shorebird Species* (2016) BirdLife Australia.

https://www.environment.gov.au/system/files/resources/da31ad38-f874-4746-a971-5510527694a4/files/revision-east-asian-australasian-flyway-population-sept-2016.pdf

Higgins, P. J. & Davies J. N. (eds.) *Handbook of Australian, New Zealand & Antarctic Birds,* vol. 3 Snipe to Pigeons (1996) Oxford University Press, Melbourne.

Pratt, H. D., Bruner, P. L., & Berrett, D. G. *The Birds of Hawaii and the Tropical Pacific* (1987) Princeton.

Rand, A. L. & Gilliard, E. T. *Handbook of New Guinea Birds* (1967) Weidenfeld & Nicolson, London.

Rand, A. L. 'Results of the Archbold Expeditions. No. 43, Birds of the 1938–1939 New Guinea Expedition.' (1942) *Bull. Amer. Mus. Hist.* 79: 425–515.

Geering, A., Agnew, L., & Harding. *Shorebirds of Australia* (2007) CSIRO Publishing, Collingwood.

Website of Latham's Snipe Project:

https://lathamssnipeproject.wordpress.com/author/geethansen/

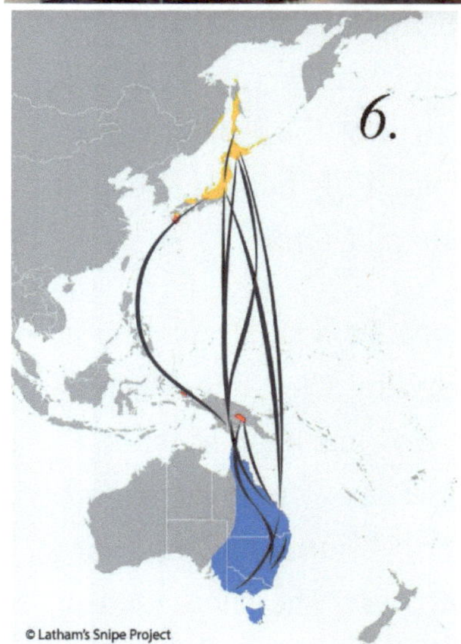

1. The fox that bit me.
2. Flying fox with young, Commonwealth Park, Canberra.
3, 4. Koel nestling, to leave for New Guinea in a few months.
5. Latham's Snipe, Canberra.
6. Snipe migration tracking results as at August 2021, map courtesy of Birgita Hansen. Note New Guinea connection.

XXII

The strange story of Ellis Rowan in New Guinea

The National Library of Australia holds 919 paintings by Ellis Rowan (1848–1922). Most of these are of wildflowers, for which Ellis is much admired. In her later years, the artist made two visits to New Guinea, during World War I, after Australian forces had overrun the German coastal settlements in what later became the Australian 'Territory of New Guinea' under a League of Nations Mandate. There are more than 80 bird paintings in the collection, all but a few being of species found in New Guinea. Ellis herself attached importance to her bird of paradise paintings, and so does the National Library.

In 2020, the same year it published a new biography, the NLA opened a small exhibition with a selection of the bird of paradise paintings. The biography, by Christine Morton-Evans, said that by the end of her second New Guinea visit ER 'had managed to paint 45 of the 52 known species of birds of paradise'. That claim echoes the entry in the *Australian Dictionary of Biography* by another biographer, Margaret Hazzard: 'Travelling only with local guides and living in primitive conditions in unmapped territory, she succeeded in painting forty-seven of the fifty-two known species, setting the birds free afterwards.'

There had been similar claims when Ellis was alive. (She died in 1922, at the age of 74.) The catalogue for an exhibition in Melbourne in November 1918 (in progress on the day of the armistice in Europe) mentioned '40 birds of paradise' (not for sale), with the note:

> This Collection of Paintings of New Guinea Birds of Paradise and Flowers is regarded as probably one of the most valuable of its kind in the world. It is the first time the subjects have been painted from actual life.

A newspaper report of a larger, final exhibition, in Sydney in March 1920, included:

> All of Mrs Rowan's birds, except six, touched up on this side afterwards, were from life on the spot. Some of these glorious birds, of the 55 known varieties of which she has painted 45, came from the Mount Bismarck Ranges (15,000 feet high).

When I visited the NLA exhibition in January 2021, it struck me as extremely unlikely that Ellis could have painted all, or even most, of the species shown where they occurred. There would have been severe difficulties at the time in travelling to the relevant locations, even for an energetic and resourceful explorer. Some would have been impossible. I devoted several weeks in 2021 to investigating the mystery of ER's pursuit of the birds of paradise. As a first step, it is not easy to work out how many species regarded as 'birds of paradise' were in the collection bought by the Commonwealth. Only a few paintings were labelled, and no inventory was included.

Despite claims in various places that Ellis had travelled extensively in unmapped parts of New Guinea, it appears that most, if not all, of the painting from life took place over some weeks at a German mission station. This was a few kilometres from the port of Madang, renamed from the German 'Friedrich-Wilhemshafen', on the north coast of the island. The artist was transported from Madang first by canoe, and then enabled to reach the hilltop mission (at a height of 350 metres) by being carried in a hammock. There is no convincing evidence that she proceeded any further to the interior of New Guinea.

Suggestions that the birds she painted were brought to her from great distances are not credible, given (a) the extreme distances to the only places some species occur, (b) the inhospitable elevations to be reached, (c) the different language speakers, unknown to one another, in the intervening spaces, and (d) the inability of later ornithologists, with skilled assistants, to collect such a range of species in the relevant area. The collectors included Tom Gilliard and Jared Diamond. Among 230 species recorded over the years in the general area were only 10 bird of paradise species.

Another biographer, Patricia Fullerton, mentions that in January 1918, ER had sought access to stuffed birds of paradise in the museum in Melbourne. In a letter to the museum for that purpose, ER said that, after some time painting from specimens in the museum in Sydney, she was, to that point, 'not able to get more than 20 of these'.

It is clear enough some of ER's pictures were copied from lithographs that had been published in books that would have been available in the State Library of Victoria. A spectacular Ellis Rowan picture that is often chosen for reproduction is labelled 'Rothschild's *Astrapia* (*Astrapia rothschildi*)' in the NLA catalogue. However, with the help of book illustrations now available this can be seen to be Arfak Astrapia, *Astrapia nigra*, a species confined to remote mountains in the extreme west of the island of New Guinea. The original was a lithograph in the 1873 *Monograph* of Daniel Giraud Elliot, from a drawing by Joseph Wolf.

In her attempt to present as many bird of paradise species as possible, ER copied illustrations of examples now known to be hybrids, as well as creating images that resemble no known reported specimen. An example of a hybrid is the '*Epimachus ellioti*' copied from the Joseph Wolf plate in Elliot's *Monograph*. There are two versions of this in the NLA collection. A picture of an unusual bird with two elongated, metallic green tail feathers seems to be an attempt to present 'Bensbach's Rifle Bird' an apparent hybrid known from a single specimen obtained by a Dutch official in the extreme west of the island of New Guinea. The original is a lithograph in the *Monograph* of Bowdler Sharpe.

In examining the contribution of Ellis Rowan to bird of paradise art, I probably spent too much time going over the online pictures and the originals in the National Library. However, I found intriguing the sketchy accounts of what Ellis was doing at that moment in time in little-known New Guinea. Whose curiosity would not be aroused by this passage in an art dealer's catalogue:

> In 1916, and again in 1917, Rowan travelled to New Guinea to paint the native flora and birds of paradise for a series of designs for the Royal Worcester Porcelain Company. In the course of these two expeditions, she documented all of the fifty-two species of birds of paradise. On these trips, she stayed at Madang Mission House on the north coast, where the missionary arranged for her to be carried in a hammock around the island by her guides, fearing that a white woman might not be safe.

Or by this, in a biographical note in 1988:

> On this journey, wracked by illness, she explored up the hazardous Ramu River in a dugout, and through the almost impenetrable Bismarck Ranges as far as Nobonob, the furthest outpost of white exploration.

I have dealt with this matter in more detail in a manuscript that I intend to lodge somewhere for the benefit of anyone who might be inclined to venture down the same road. The year 2022 marked 100 years from the passing of Ellis Rowan, a remarkable traveller and artist, whatever the true story behind her birds of paradise.

The story of Ellis Rowan is also an occasion to mention those books she made use of. They belong to that great period in the 19th century of large books illustrating strange birds, many for the first time:

Elliot, D. G. (1873) *A Monograph of the Paradiseidae or Birds of Paradise.* Printed for the subscribers by the author. https://www.biodiversitylibrary.org/item/156590#page/1/mode/1up

Gould, J., completed by Sharpe, B. S. (1875-1888) *The Birds of New Guinea and the Adjacent Papuan Islands.* Henry Sotheran, London. https://www.biodiversitylibrary.org/item/229855#page/7/mode/1up

Sharpe, B. S. (1891-1898) *Monograph of the Paradiseidae or Birds of Paradise and Ptilonorhynchidae or Bower-birds.* Henry Sotheran, London. https://www.biodiversitylibrary.org/item/191510#page/1/mode/1up

An unusual bringing together of birds, books, blossoms and fashion. In early 2021, the National Library of Australia had a display of Ellis Rowan's bird of paradise pictures from the library collection. During this, an exhibition outside the library bookshop showed some of the watercolours together with Nicky Zimmermann dress designs inspired by Ellis. Arrow indicates an Ellis BoP pic.

Some points about Ellis Rowan's bird art from First World War New Guinea.

At right is an Ellis Rowan picture sometimes reproduced
as 'Rothschild's Bird of Paradise'. It appears to have
been copied from Joseph Wolf's lithograph (below) of
Astrapia nigra, a rare species from the Vogelkop
Peninsula in former Dutch New Guinea.   At bottom left
is one of two similar images in the NLA Ellis Rowan
Collection. It appears to be copied from the Joseph Wolf
lithograph beside it.   If so, it is a very rare hybrid, once
known as 'Elliot's Bird of Paradise.' The curious bird in
the centre might be modelled on a lithograph of
'Bensbach's Bird of Paradise'.

'Bensbach's Bird of
Paradise', known from a
single specimen.
(Keulemans & Hart lith.))

134

XXIII

The intermittently elusive Gang-gang and the advancing Koel

For me, the Gang-gang was a childhood species. I would occasionally see small flocks around Geelong. Charles Belcher (*Birds of the District of Geelong* (1914)) said they appeared around the town from March to October. They came out of the forest to open country from the direction of the Otways, at irregular periods, and not every year. He mentions not less than 50 birds, in 1913, at Eastern Park. I saw them in Eastern Park, too, more than once, only about a half-dozen birds. They were quite mobile, so people argued about whether reports from different places were of just the one flock. The regular appearance of the species around Canberra follows a similar pattern, although not so strictly seasonal. For what is regarded as a common species, it can be hard to find when you need to, for an overseas visitor for example – or for someone from Queensland.

I associate Gang-gangs with suburban parks and gardens and street trees. In Canberra, there is a variety of eucalypts which offer a choice of seed capsules. A Broad-leaved Peppermint I planted on the street verge sometimes attracts a feeding group. They are very fond of seeds of certain kinds of exotic trees, including some kinds of hawthorn. Like other cockatoos and parrots, they eat leaves of the introduced African Boxthorn.

Among the occasions I have been unable to produce a Gang-gang on request was the visit in 2006 of David Bird, of *The Bird Almanac* (revised and updated, 2004). This useful book contains a lot of information about birds that you might not need, but, if you do need it, you will not find easily anywhere else. One section lists 'records in the bird world', including in the matter of anatomy. A couple of local birds do quite well here. The 'absolute longest bill' belongs to 'Australian pelican at 47cm (18.5in)'. The 'longest legs relative to body length' are attached to 'black-winged stilt at 23 cm (9 in) or 60% of its height'. Some might raise the quibble that our Pied Stilt has been split from *H. himantopus*. Perhaps so, but I am yet to be convinced that our stilts are not the ones with the bird world's longest legs (relative to body length).

135

A Gang-gang is on the cover of Neil Hermes book about birds of Canberra and the high country.
The bird is splitting hawthorn berries to gain access to the tiny seeds.

Another Gang-gangless occasion was when Joe Forshaw brought around Bill and Wendy Cooper to renew their acquaintance with the species. Of course, the birds were around the day before, but not when they were wanted. Probably the best way to get an almost-guaranteed sighting is to check with people who have them at feeders. Even then, they are likely to be reliably present only at certain times of day and times of year.

Across all regions, as the landscape changes, new bird species appear while others decline. I mention here one particular species. It is found in Canberra, but I have come across it elsewhere. It is a summer visitor from New Guinea, at home in the suburbs, particularly established leafy ones. It is known as the Eastern or Pacific Koel, *Eudynamis orientalis*. It is likely to remain 'Eastern or Pacific Koel' for some time, as the preference of each school for its chosen English name rests on a deeply held certainty about the correctness of its position. If I look in eBird for the 'English (Australia)' name' of 'Eastern Koel' I am advised there are 'no matches'. I do better with 'Pacific Koel'.

The species is now recorded south to Melbourne and Geelong, and beyond. Its regular appearance around Canberra in the warmer months is to me one of the most noticeable changes, since about 2008, in the local bird scene. It is a noisy bird. Sometimes there are more plaintive 'ko-eels', sometimes more excited 'wirra-wirras', and sometimes the 'kek-ek-eks' are more frequent. Around Canberra, the females lay eggs in nests of the Red Wattlebird. Usually from December there are many reports of the dependent young as they urge on their over-worked foster parents with a regular, monotonous 'eep … eep … eep'.

An energetic COG member, Jack Holland, has kept records in recent seasons of all dependent young brought to his attention. He has tried to avoid double-counting, but still believes his totals represent only a small proportion of actual fledglings. The young recorded in Canberra suburbs were: 2017 – 86; 2018 – 87; 2019 – 69. (And see my final chapter for an update on this trend.) These are significant numbers given that only a few years earlier there were no such records. Perhaps numbers will decline if the wattlebird hosts become less naïve, or if numbers of breeding wattlebirds are reduced. That species is also suffering from another trend, increasing numbers of aggressive Noisy Miners, a medium-large honeyeater that is taking over some suburban areas.

Persistent calling by male koels has caused the species to enter the consciousness of many Canberrans who would not usually claim an interest in birds. A section of the community, which included a local politician, took the position that the species was a 'pest', and therefore a candidate for extermination. That view might have been encouraged by publicity for a campaign to exterminate, or sharply reduce, the local population of the Common Myna (an introduced starling relative, not a honeyeater). The anti-koel move was blunted, if not laid completely to rest, by the news that the koel was a native species, and therefore entitled to share our neighbourhood. Many people still dislike it. For some people, the koel might seem to be one of the darker forces of nature, being heard but rarely seen, perhaps suggesting some kind of affiliation with the bunyip of scary childhood stories.

I have mentioned our daughter Serin, now resident in Cambridge, UK. Evidently pleased with her own bird name, she decided to continue the fashion with her own children, two boys. One is named 'Koel', the other 'Raile'. To learn the reasoning behind those choices you would need to ask Serin.

The Gang-gang Cockatoo is a familiar emblematic
Canberra species . The bird at right is feeding in a
street eucalypt.   Among visitors seeking a view of one
without success was Canadian David Bird of the *Bird
Almanac*. However, two other Canberra species
(shown) have gained inclusion in the *Almanac's*
record list - for relative leg length and bill size.

Bill and Wendy Cooper also failed to renew
acquaintance with the species, even with the help of
Joe Forshaw. The birds have been added to the scene.

XXIV

The end of certainty

A bird in the hand is a certainty, but a bird in the bush may sing.
—Bret Harte

We suggest that a revised taxonomy that better captures avian species diversity will enhance the quantification and analysis of global patterns of diversity and distribution as well as provide a more appropriate framework for understanding the evolutionary history of birds.
—Barrowclough, G. F., Cracraft J., Klicka J., and Zink R. M., 2016

Where have all the flowers gone?
—Song by Pete Seeger, 1955

Among the many things that have become uncertain, I mention here three that concern birds. First, what has happened to species? Second, what are their names? Third, what is happening to them?

What is certainty? If, for present purposes, it is to be represented by a bird book, it might be the *Reader's Digest Complete Book of Australian Birds,* first published 1976, revised edition 1986. In many Australian homes this volume, too large for the average book-case, sat on a shelf waiting to be consulted for anything you needed to know about birds. It was like a trusted dictionary, or perhaps a favourite cookery book, or a bible (or equivalent, depending on the religious tradition of the household). Reviewing the first edition in *Emu,* Simon Bennett wrote: 'The text accurately summarises much that is known of Australian birds. The list of contributors is like a *Who's Who* of Australian ornithology ...'. The revised edition was edited by Dick Schodde and Sonia Tidemann.

Today, more people than ever are out looking for birds. For a lot of them the aim is to see as many different species as possible. Therefore, it is a matter of some importance to them whether they are seeing species X or species Y, in fact, more basically, what a species is. Fortunately, they need not worry about deciding that matter for themselves. They are given that information by a checklist, or by a field guide based on a 'checklist'.

There are now different global checklists which vary in their details according to editorial decisions whether to accept proposals for changes published by scientists working in their specialised corners of the bird world. Some disagreement is to be expected, but this is now more fundamental with the growing use of genetic information drawn from looking at DNA samples. That information, it is said, provides a better basis for understanding how species have evolved than grouping them according to more obvious differences and similarities.

In my *Living Birds of the World*, E Thomas Gilliard had said there were about 8600 species of birds. A paper was published in 2016 by George Barrowclough and others entitled 'How Many Kinds of Bird Are There and Why Does It Matter?'[4]. This argued that the number of bird species had been 'significantly underestimated due to a taxonomic tradition not found in most other taxonomic groups'. Using genetic data, it was calculated that the species diversity of birds had been underestimated by 'current taxonomy' by at least a factor of two. The paper put forward a new figure of 18, 043 bird species worldwide.

Without necessarily accepting that number of bird species, we have reached the stage where genetic information sometimes suggests a different conclusion as to species separation from the traditional pointers, such as plumage features. That difference of approach was sharpened when the Cambridge-based Birdlife International, primarily a conservation body, adopted an approach based on a refinement of the 'traditional pointers', including voice. Known as the 'Tobias criteria', that approach was intended to be of more practical use in developing countries. It rejected use of genetic information as a main criterion.

The BLI approach is described in some detail in the introductions by Nigel Collar to the two *Checklist* volumes published jointly by BLI and the *Handbook of the Birds of the World* (2014, 2016). The present Birdlife Australia approach, and list, is aligned with that of BLI, its partner organisation. On the other hand, a short practical account of the gene-based approach is given by Leo Joseph in the *Australian Bird Guide* (P. Menkhorst and others), a field guide adopting a list that generally follows that perspective. Given that there are surprisingly few differences as regards species recognized, the two approaches can be regarded as different ways of getting to a similar result, together with, one suspects, a certain amount of restraint to avoid too much divergence.

---

[4] https://journals.plos.org/plosone/article?id=10.1371/journal.pone.0166307

Currently, work is in progress to produce a single unified world checklist. If successful, this will be convenient for birdwatchers. However, it seems unlikely that such a list will form an agreed starting point for future scientific work. It will not answer, for everyone, the question 'What is a species?'

In a recent article on speciation by Leo Joseph, a 'lay summary' was provided. The first sentence is: 'Biologists still debate what species are and how we should best demarcate one species from another.'[5] A single world checklist will not end that debate.

In many discussions of species limits, there is at least a reference to 'implications for conservation'. It is often pointed out, not convincingly some might think, that the species distinction is not all that important. This is because conservation measures can be directed to a genetic unit below the level of species, such as a subspecies or a population (see Chapter XVII above). This seems to me to introduce yet more room for debate into a complicated issue. In the end, most people will think that species are the important thing.

My second uncertainty concerns the English names we use for birds. For Australia, the work of the English Names Committee has been discussed above. That committee was set up with a conservative mandate, part of a system intended to defend, for better or worse, the English names settled on in the period 1975 to 1984. After that, those who'd taken part had had enough of arguments about names. For some names, in default of agreement, a plebiscite had been needed to put an end to the debate. Stability was seen as an important principle in names policy.

In recent years, some people are saying they are not convinced by the stability argument and see reasons to question many of the English names used by BirdLife Australia. The main target at present is eponymous names, that is names that refer to a person. Initially, the concern was particular names that referred to a person associated with misconduct of some kind, for example 'Major Mitchell's Cockatoo'. More recently, we have seen a move to eliminate all eponymous names, following a similar move in North America:

> Eponymous common names are essentially verbal statues. They were made to honor the benefactor in perpetuity, and as such reflect the accomplishments and values that the creator esteemed. We are not bound by either the intention or the regard; we should make decisions about who and what we honor based on our own values, values that create a more equitable world for all. By continuing to use

---

[5] *American Ornithology* 2021, vol. 138, 1–15

eponymous common bird names, we continue to reference and honor our distressful colonial heritage and the racism that was a direct consequence of this malicious exploitation. This is unacceptable, and we must do better. (*Bird Names for Birds* https://birdnamesforbirds.wordpress.com/)

A proposal tentatively adopted within BirdLife Australia at the time of writing would call for replacement of all eponymous names for Australian bird species and subspecies. This would involve quite a few changes. For example, the unfortunate 'King Parrot' would again require renaming. This has been Tabuan Parrot, Governor King's Parrot, King Lory, and Australian King-Parrot. Perhaps we shall see a reversion to 'Scarlet and Green Parrot', the name used by John Latham in 1801.

Governor King's Parrot, more or less. Still in need of a settled name.

Another call for revision of English names comes from a different direction. Many observers in Australia, and some regional bodies, use a global bird list which adopts a different English name, one that is more appropriate from an international perspective. Thus 'Maned Duck' is coming back, and 'Myzomela' is being widely used. So it would be 'Scarlet Myzomela' instead of 'Scarlet Honeyeater'. There is no longer one 'correct' name.

My third uncertainty concerns the actual birds that are out there, or, more particularly, what is happening to them. Apart from migration, the numbers of a particular bird species in a particular area are likely to ebb and flow, usually ebb, unfortunately. *The New Atlas of Australian Birds* (Birds Australia, 2003) compared numbers with the results of an earlier atlas. Lists were given of increasers and decliners, together with maps showing where the increasing or declining had taken place.

From my own experience of 40 years in Canberra, I know that the Crested Pigeon has progressed from a rarity on the fringes of the city to abundant in most suburbs. The Superb Parrot has grown in local numbers. The Regent Honeyeater has become extremely rare. The

Noisy Miner has become a dominant woodland species, excluding several small species. Brown Treecreepers are disappearing. The most spectacular increaser is the Eastern Koel, the migratory cuckoo that arrives each year from the tropics. The first breeding record in Canberra was in 2008/2009 (*Canberra Bird Notes* 34 (2), June 2009). I have already mentioned the work of Jack Holland in keeping track of fledgling numbers. The latest news is that in the 2020/2021 season an astonishing 365 were counted, over four times more than in any previous season. One can only wonder what is going on with that species.

Until recently those kinds of fluctuations in bird numbers (may I call them 'routine'?) have been generally attributed to deliberate or incidental human-caused changes to the landscape, in particular land clearing and (relevant to the koel) the planting of new kinds of vegetation. Now we have the Great Uncertainty of climate change. 'Is global warming affecting the birds?', people ask. There is some evidence about that, and a lot of speculation based on apparent changes in distribution. There is no point giving examples here. Simply put 'birds climate change' in your digital search engine.

A Sulphur-crested Cockatoo and an Australian Magpie, each with the early-morning sun in a smoke-filled sky, during the bushfires of December 2019, which approached Canberra.

Appendix

The 'Ebird' dimension: Digital excursions

These days if you are making a list of birds in a strange place you may not need a hard copy field guide, or even need to know where you are. Your phone tells you that, and what the bird looks like and sounds like. It also keeps your records.

A popular recording system is eBird, managed by the Cornell Lab of Ornithology. That organisation also manages a *Birds of the World* information source covering 10,721 species, and a Macaulay Library with over 21 million photographic, video and audio records. EBird holds over 800 million observations. Although I am a poor recorder, I can only admire the dedication of the thousands who have contributed to this trove of information. In consulting eBird to learn what birds have been observed, and where, you need to bear in mind that only some people contribute to it (I don't), that people who do might not submit all their observations, and that some observations might be suppressed for one reason or other. EBird is more used in some parts of the world than others. To investigate some of the bird species I have referred to in the early chapters above, we can check into eBird (as in January 2021) to see what observations have been reported.

The Song Thrush in Australia. The pockets where you can find this introduction have not expanded much. EBird reports suggest the mainland population in Australia is limited to Victoria, mainly around Port Phillip Bay, and in the Otways. It is found also on Lord Howe and Norfolk Islands.

Singing Starling. Widely reported across PNG, particularly Port Moresby, and the Solomons. Reports from Boigu Island seem to depend on visits by travelling eBirders, so not recorded since March 2020.

Oriental Pratincole. Many records in northern Australia, but a bird of irregular occurrence further south. No eBird records in Papua New Guinea in last 10 years.

Cnemophilus macregorii. Now 'Crested Satinbird'. This was the 'bird of paradise' photographed by Loke Wan Tho in 1952, near Nondugl. It must be recognized that only small parts of PNG, generally at or near main centres, have been covered in eBird reports. In the last 10 years, there has been a sprinkling of reports of this species further west near Mount Hagen and further west again around Kumul Lodge on the road to Wabag. There are no eBird records since 2019. There is a single 1988 report from Varirata National Park near Port Moresby, and one at higher altitude, on the Kokoda Trail, in 1987.

Nearest reports to Port Moresby of the Raggiana Bird of Paradise, P. raggiana. The species is associated with wet forest. There is a 1983 report of five at Pacific Adventist University about 8 km from Port Moresby airport, and a 2017 report of six about 6 km further along the road to Varirata, at the beginning of the Laloki Gorge. So far this year there is a single report at Varirata, in March. There are several records, presumably from tourists, along the Kokoda Trail, near Kokoda itself.

Magnificent Riflebird. The absence of eBird reports from the Port Moresby area is explained by a taxonomic change. The species in eastern PNG is now the Growling Riflebird *P. intercedens*, a species not shared with Australia. There are a few reports of this new bird of paradise from the forest country just beyond Port Moresby.

Purple Heron in Italy. It seems central Italy is not the heartland of this species. In fact, its occurrence there is quite spotty. There is an eBird record at Lago Fibreno Riserva Naturale about 30 km from Lago di Scanno.

Great Bustard. The Burgenland area of Austria has many records of this species, one concentration being near the Hungarian border.

Upland Sandpiper. There is an eBird record of this species at Dover Air Force Base in August 2020. However, appearance there is intermittent, only every few years. Cape May on the other side of Delaware Bay, a famous site for bird migration, has more records, but again only every few years.

Whooping Crane. Alas, the days of the Whooping Cranes at Bosque de Apaches seem to be over. There is a long sequence of sightings from 1976, through the 1980s when my brief visit occurred, but none since January 2001. There are now many sightings along the more traditional flight paths further east, with southern end-points in Texas and Florida.

Wood Warbler migration. In eBird, you can pick a day in spring and click on any promising hotspot in Montgomery County, in Maryland, just north of the DC boundary. One observer on 29 April 2016 has 10 warbler species including Northern Waterthrush and American Redstart. Another on 5 May 2012 also has 10 in a slightly different list including Ovenbird, Northern Parula and Prairie Warbler.

Spiny Babbler. Turdoides (Acanthoptila) nipalensis. This is not so hard to find, after all. There are many eBird reports of this species, from various locations in Nepal, although it remains confined to that country. It can be found in the vicinity of Kathmandu itself. Its conservation status is 'Least Concern'.

Pink-headed Duck. There are only two reports in eBird, both in the Indian state of Bihar, both by Charles McFarlane Inglis ('Posthumous'). They are dated 1904 (kept in aviary) and 1935 (courtesy of the Inglis retriever). A recent book (*HBW/BLI Checklist*) says 'Last acceptable record in the wild from 1949; a possible recent sighting (2004) and credible local reports (2005) from N Myanmar'. The reference is to *Bird Conserv. Int.* 18(1): 38–52.

Abbreviations

ACT	Australian Capital Territory
ANU	Australian National University
ANWC	Australian National Wildlife Collection
BLA	Birdlife Australia
BLI	Birdlife International
COG	Canberra Ornithologists Group
CSIRO	Commonwealth Scientific & Industrial Research Organisation
eBird	A digital recording system administered by Cornell Lab
NAIDOC	National Aborigines and Islanders Day Observance Committee
NLA	National Library of Australia
NSW	New South Wales (an Australian State)
PNG	Papua New Guinea
RAOU	Royal Australasian Ornithologists Union (predecessor to BLA)